A Midlands Odyssey

A Midlands Odyssey

Edited by Polly Stoker, Elisabeth Charis and Jonathan Davidson

ISBN: 978-0-9927589-8-1

Cover photograph © Eleanor Bennett
www.eleanorleonnebennett.zenfolio.com

First published October 2014 by:

Nine Arches Press
PO Box 6269
Rugby
CV21 9NL

www.ninearchespress.com

Printed in Britain by:

imprintdigital.net
Seychelles Farm,
Upton Pyne,
Exeter
EX5 5HY
www.imprintdigital.net

A Midlands Odyssey

Edited by Polly Stoker, Elisabeth Charis and Jonathan Davidson

Nine
Arches
Press

A Midlands Odyssey is a Writing West Midlands / Birmingham Literature Festival project managed by Owl Productions.

We gratefully acknowledge the support of the Arts and Humanities Research Council and the Archive of Performances of Greek and Roman Drama for this project.

CONTENTS

INTRODUCTION

THIS COLLECTION of ten responses to the *Odyssey*, one of two ancient Greek epics attributed to Homer, emerges at a time of immense popular interest in the myth, literature and thought of the ancient world. With formal classical education harder to come by, the dissemination of the body of texts known as Classics increasingly falls to artists and sees the opening up of literary conversations as old as the works themselves to new and divergent voices. 'Not knowing Greek', a thorn in the side of Woolf and Keats, is no longer an obstacle to participation in the transmission of texts like the *Odyssey*, as this collection bears out. Those previously disenfranchised from classical learning on the basis of gender, class and ethnicity are now at the forefront of classical reception, endowing ancient literature with new life and challenging Classics' traditional elitism. Of course, the practices of revision, appropriation and versioning are nothing new but the sheer volume and variety of contemporary engagements with the ancient world is remarkable, something that this collection is both a product and a new example of.

Precisely why artists return, time and again, to these ancient stories is a compelling question but one without a definitive answer. The idea that the longevity of these texts lies in their saying something universal about mankind is simply too easy an explanation, and often neglects the very specific and deliberate ways in which different times and places read and recreate these works anew. Explicitly 'situated' in the Midlands, for example, our collection forms part of a longstanding tradition of epic storytelling while simultaneously remaining local and of its time. It is perhaps more helpful to think about recurring themes and images that may characterise a 'moment' of reception. If we reflect on the mechanics of the writing process, drawing on the relationship between the old text and its reincarnations, important questions emerge that are key to thinking about the interplay between the ancient and the contemporary. Where does the *Odyssey* end and the new work begin? When we read a piece from the collection, whose voice are we hearing; that of Homer, the author or a melding of the two? What is Homeric about these retellings; is reception in a word or phrase, an image or theme?

Our anthology is certainly striking for its lack of violence, a noticeable contrast to the *Odyssey*; the suffering here tending to be internal and cerebral as opposed to bodily. With graphic images of atrocities channelled directly to us every day on our television screens and over the internet, is there a sense in which fantastical representations of suffering, such as we find in Homer, are in bad taste; at best, inadequate and at worst, offensive?

Moments of humour and lightness do feature throughout the collection but it is a recurrent sadness and pathos that emerges most profoundly and it is in this way that our contemporary receptions most clearly meet and build upon their ancient model. Whilst reminding us that the *Odyssey* is a story of loss and waste, there is a complementary thread of interpretation that sees this world-weariness as something equally appropriate to the here and now. It has been suggested, for example, that the sense of defeat emanating from some of our anthology's characters may be redolent of a Midlands identity. What does this say about the place of the epic and its hero in the 21st century and would it even be possible to approach the *Odyssey* now without one's reading being coloured by at least some cynicism and disillusionment?

The brief for the collection was simple: to write a short-story response to an element of Homer's *Odyssey* in a contemporary

Midlands setting. At first we envisaged allocating a different episode from the *Odyssey* to each writer but it became clear during the commissioning process that this overly 'managed' approach could not work, freeing up each writer to find their own way into the epic.

Although some retellings have a greater sense of closure and are more easily identifiable with their Homeric models than others, there is an overriding coherence to the pieces where, much like the ancient text itself, potentially separate stories come together to create a unified whole. Our anthology is in no way claiming to retell Homer's *Odyssey* in its entirety nor to fully represent a region as complex and diverse as the Midlands. We hope instead that it is not too ambitious to anticipate that what we have produced here are ten episodes in the story that, over time, may be told as *A Midlands Odyssey*.

POLLY STOKER AND **ELISABETH CHARIS**

YASMIN ALI

In the Lap of the Gods

Eddie walked through the car factory for the last time. His work here was nearly done.

'You've seen my draft report to Frankfurt,' said Eddie to the plant manager at his side. 'We have two options. Both lead to productivity gains, one's going to hurt more. What's your take on this, Salim?'

'Real technical innovation? That means job losses,' said Salim. 'But Turkey has enough history. We need to protect the future. We're a young country.'

'Good man,' said Eddie, with a collusive nod. The phone pulsed in his pocket, but he chose to ignore it. In any case, he could guess who it was. Athene.

At the Athene offices Claire could scarcely contain her excitement. 'I just know they're going to love this,' she said.

'Maybe,' said David, 'but Poseidon's after it, too. Don't write them off. They sunk our last bid to Channel Four.'

'But it's not Channel Four, is it? This is Zeus,' said Claire. 'They want bold, edgy…'

'They want ratings,' said David. 'Eyes on the prize, remember?'

So it was that Claire came to prepare for her meeting with the Commissioning Editor (Factual) at Zeus Television. The meeting took place at his club. The Olympus drew little attention to itself from the street; just a discreet doorway in

Soho marked by a simple aluminium plate. Inside was a little different. A flunky dressed like a spangly Seventies game show host showed Claire up to the first floor library where Jolyon sat in a flamboyantly upholstered armchair reading on his tablet.

'It's a street in Birmingham,' said Claire.

'Benefits Street. It's been done,' said Jolyon. 'Poverty porn, too depressing.'

'This has got wealth and poverty, freaks and glamour,' Claire began.

'Heartbreak and humour?' said Jolyon.

'Check,' said Claire. 'Really. It has everything.'

'Death?' said Jolyon.

'Absolutely,' said Claire. 'Athene are confident that this series reinvents reality television.'

'So,' said Jolyon, picking imaginary fluff from the knee of his burgundy trousers and dropping it to the floor. The gesture warned Claire that she was losing his attention. 'Give me the pitch in one word.'

'War,' said Claire.

Jolyon looked up from contemplation of his finger nails. 'OK. A sentence.'

'Our cast have all been touched by war – profoundly,' said Claire.

'What war?'

'War,' said Claire. 'Falklands, Balkans, Gulf, Libya. We've even got an old couple who fled Belfast in the 1970s and ended up losing their friends in the IRA pub bombing.'

'I see the heartbreak,' said Jolyon. 'But where's the humour? More to the point, where's the glamour? And they're all on one street?'

'Around it. Bristol Road,' said Claire. 'It's quite long.'

'Let's eat,' said Jolyon. 'I'm not sold on this, but I'm interested. I'll hear you out.'

The walk to the dining room gave Claire the charge of energy she needed. Olympus members and their guests noted

Jolyon. His aura was tangible. A red-top editor nodded, a fashionable writer stopped Jolyon for a quiet word, a BBC executive, no doubt looking for a route out of exile to Salford, air kissed the man. His power was a forcefield that took in his companion. The envious eyes of Claire's peers and rivals took note. Athene Productions was one to watch.

At the table, the best table, supplicants approached to remind the man from Zeus of projects pending, and pitches proposed. An act from the theatre of power, this ended when Jolyon's body language signalled that lunch had been ordered, and negotiations were about to begin.

'The story?' said Jolyon.

'OK,' said Claire. 'We've people with PTSD, refugees, exiles, fighters, victims. But they've found a way through their experiences. They're real characters.'

'Characters, maybe, but where's the story.'

'The arc centres on one family,' said Claire.

'Are they British?' said Jolyon. 'Our audience need people they can identify with.'

'Yes,' said Claire. 'From that longest of British wars, the class war.'

Jolyon spluttered, and reached for his glass. 'Did you say "class war"?'

'It's the conflict at the heart of this series,' said Claire. 'It binds everything together. Birmingham used to be the centre of the motor industry. I've got a guy who worked at Longbridge all his life.'

'Long bridge?' said Jolyon.

'Car factory at the end of our road,' said Claire. 'Or, at least it used to be. Synonymous with industrial militancy back in the day. Our old guy was a communist. Retired on a final salary pension and moved to a nice bungalow.'

'Communist is exotic,' said Jolyon, 'but I'm hearing too much 'old'. Not sure that works for our demographic.'

'There's a mid-century *moderne* angle,' said Claire.' The

guy worked on the original Issigonis Mini.'

'Niche,' said Jolyon.

'Just a detail,' said Claire. 'The old man's son was apprenticed to British Leyland, too, as it was called by then. That's Eddie. He fought the management, too. Lost his job, lost his pension...'

'So?' said Jolyon.

'Lost his family,' said Claire. 'Had to move to find work. At first he commuted to Cowley. Then he worked at the Honda plant at Swindon. His marriage fell apart, leaving the wife behind with her baby son, Tel, but Eddie drifted on. Up to Nissan in Sunderland. On to the Czech Republic to help VW take over Skoda.'

'I'm losing the plot,' said Jolyon. 'How does any of this make for reality television?'

'It's back-story, I know,' said Claire. 'But believe me, it works. Eddie's ex-wife, Penny, still lives near Eddie's dad. She's done all right for herself. Took the license on a pub. Used to be a spit-'n-sawdust place for car workers. Now it's a smart gastropub full of young professionals.'

'This is beginning to sound like some kind of anthropological study,' said Jolyon. 'Benefits Street, I get. Made In Chelsea, TOWIE. But what is this?'

'The back story's important,' said Claire. 'What we want to do, across the arc of this series, is bring Eddie back. To reunite him with his dad, his son. Maybe even his wife. End the class war with a romantic meal in Penny's bistro.'

'Best laid plans. What if all hell breaks loose?' said Jolyon.

'We can handle that,' said Claire.

It had taken some careful positioning to beat Poseidon to the Zeus commission, but Claire and her colleagues were determined to make this series Athene's calling card in the business. Now all they had to do was make the programmes.

Izzy the intern rented flats for the crew in the Rotunda,

a converted office building near the Bull Ring that was once the distinctive centre of the Birmingham skyline. Researchers armed with notes from Claire and David charmed the 'cast' and solicited the permissions. Claire herself worked on Eddie's family. With their help, she felt, this project could be epic.

First, she visited Len, Eddie's elderly father.

'Come in, bab,' said Len, answering the door of his neat bungalow. 'Nice to see a pretty face.'

Len basked in Claire's attention. She listened intently to his tales of working with Red Robbo, and made a show of taking copious notes.

'You've got great tales to tell, Len,' said Claire. 'The stuff about your days as a shop steward is brilliant, but you must have some personal stories, too.'

'I thought this was about class war?' said Len. 'We never called it that, mind.'

'The human touch, Len,' said Claire. 'That's what helps people to engage. Like when your son joined the firm as an apprentice. You must have been proud that day, walking in to work with him.'

'I was on nights that week, bab,' said Len. 'Anyway, we took it for granted that if we had a lad he'd join us on the shop floor. ETU rules. Well, it was probably EETPU by then.'

'What was that?' said Claire. 'EPU, or something?'

'Frank Chappell's lot,' said Len. When Claire shook her head slowly, he added, 'The electricians' union.'

'But you must have been pleased Eddie wanted to work with you, family pride?,' said Claire.

'Oh, ar,' said Len. 'I've always been proud of Eddie. Did well at Shenley Court, bab. And he didn't let the battle for Longbridge defeat him. Works all over the world now. The stories he could tell you.'

'But you miss him?' said Claire.

'Can't say I don't,' said Len, 'but the lad's got his own life to lead.'

Getting Len to sign the consent forms had been easy enough. Getting him to stick to the script once they started filming was likely to be more difficult. They had cast him as a lonely old man who wants to see his son again before he dies. Still, it was all in the edit.

Penny was harder work. Claire couldn't ingratiate herself with the woman, so David tried an approach. In the flat over the pub he picked up a photograph of Penny's son.

'Is this your boy?' said David, although he knew the answer.

'Yes,' said Penny. 'Spitting image of his dad.'

'Do you find that difficult?' said David. 'The resemblance?'

'No,' said Penny. 'When Eddie went, that was difficult. They were difficult times for all of us, for the whole city.'

'What happened?' said David.

'We hadn't been married long,' said Penny. 'I mean, we'd known each other since we were kids, but after Tel was born we bought a house, mortgage, all that.'

'Then the factory closed down,' said David.

'Longbridge wasn't just a factory,' said Penny. 'Look, old people today, they still talk about the Austin. MG Rover by the time it closed, a shadow of what it had been, but to us it represented what we expected from life.'

'A job for life?' said David.

'Look at Len,' said Penny, 'from apprentice to gold watch. Birmingham people used to think that was their birthright.'

'Who do you blame for the collapse of your marriage?' said David.

'Our marriage didn't collapse,' said Penny. 'It never stood a chance. Men like Eddie. Well, he's like his dad.'

'Meaning?' said David.

'He'd gone into British Leyland as an apprentice,' said Penny. 'He wasn't a tankie like his dad, but he was Labour, a solid union man. It's how he defined himself. He couldn't have stayed with us and stacked shelves at Sainsbury's. It would have humiliated him.'

'But you were left alone with a child,' said David.

'That wasn't easy. But Eddie always paid the bills,' said Penny. 'Generously. That's how I was able to get this place. I was always financially secure.'

'And Tel,' said David. 'How's he doing now?'

'That's the irony,' said Penny. 'He's doing engineering at Bournville College. On the site of the old Longbridge plant. Like father, like son.'

'You know it's a great story,' said David. 'A strong, attractive woman, left to bring up her son alone. She becomes a successful businesswoman, the boy maintains the family trade. And it would be terrific publicity for the business.'

'That's the only reason I'm even thinking of doing this,' said Penny.

It was enough for Athene.

Eddie sat on the terrace of his Istanbul apartment with an early evening beer. He was doing a lot of thinking about the past, thanks to Athene. The television company had been astonishingly persistent. Emails, phone calls, promises of first-class travel, above all the attention of a charming young woman who had taken Skype flirting to a whole new level. Was it fate that he should return to Birmingham now? He'd been away so long. He was estranged from Penny, and scarcely knew his own son, except through the occasional photograph. A reunion would have been hard in the best of circumstances, but accompanied by a raucous television crew it might be hell.

For Athene, filming the minor stories for their series was easy. The American teenager who'd dodged the draft in the early 1970s, and now ran a chain of artisanal bakeries across the Midlands and the Cotswolds, just wanted to play the grey hipster and promote his sourdough. The Syrian student stranded far from home by war might have been too much reality for the reality genre, but with his boy-band looks and genial manner, Athene could cut him into the narrative without troubling the viewers unduly. The Somalis might have been a problem until they found an unusually tall, good looking family. The boy was already a promising basketball player, and Claire had managed to talk the daughter into going to a modelling audition where the agent had shrieked "the new Alek Wek!" Great telly.

But the multi-generational tale of Len, Eddie, Tel and the lovely Penny in her palace of a coaching inn was at the centre of the series. Len had proved to be more malleable than Claire had at first suspected. Nothing was too much trouble for the cameras.

'Can we do that again, Len?' said Claire. 'From the bit about Eddie's first day at Longbridge.'

'Alright, bab,' said Len. He coughed, raised his head confidently, and held out a photograph towards the camera. 'This,' he began, 'is my lad Eddie when he was sixteen. I was that proud when he followed me into Longbridge. We walked in together that morning as Men of the Midlands.'

'Fabulous, Len,' said Claire. She now had something she could use with the archive footage of Mitchells and Butlers beer commercials for ATV.

'Now just a few shots we can use when we cut it,' said Claire.

'In the garden again?' said Len, fancying himself something of a pro now.

'Kitchen, this time, I think,' said Claire. 'How about making a nice cup of tea?'

'Two sugars for you, Rashid?' said Len to the cameraman. To Claire he said, 'You're sweet enough, bab.'

'Can you just make the one cup?' said Claire. 'Then take it and sit down in the armchair over there.'

'Not my usual chair?' said Len.

'Believe me, that one will work better,' said Claire.

Filming in Penny's pub had gone well, too. An intern had some archive footage of the pub in the 1980s; car workers with mullets playing darts in a cramped bar. The contrast with Penny's interior was delicious. The pub was now spacious and artfully lit, with mismatched vintage armchairs and distressed leather sofas, and as for the clientele, the tables with their espresso cups and cocktail glasses told a story of different times. The host, Penny, in silk dress and heels, looked every inch the glamorous pillar of the Chamber of Commerce.

Claire had spoken to Eddie a few days earlier, and sensed that his resolve was weakening. He was trouble-shooting for Volkswagen in Turkey, but the job was coming to an end. His next contract for Tata in India wouldn't start for weeks. If they could just get him to come home it would give the series the climax they needed. She called him again.

'You have no excuse,' said Claire, smiling, to the image on her tablet.

'I haven't been to Birmingham for years,' said Eddie, gazing out at the container ships heading down the Bosphorus. 'I know I'll go back some time, see my family. But I'm not sure this is the right way to do it.'

'Really, this is perfect. We bring you back,' said Claire. 'At Athene's expense. What's not to like?' Eddie's expression suggested that there was plenty not to like. 'Let me tell you something, Your dad's having a great time with the cameras. It's rejuvenated him. And he's a natural. I'll send you some of the rushes, see what you think.'

Claire had already edited the sequence she intended to send to Eddie. She composed a friendly email, attached the file and pressed 'send'.

The sun was setting as Eddie contemplated opening the file. He needed a second beer before he felt able to look at what they'd sent. He propped up his tablet and with some wariness, opened the file.

Eddie relaxed as the sequence began. Len was talking about his time in the motor industry, and his pride at being followed into it by his clever son who went straight from school to an engineering apprenticeship at Longbridge. Eddie smiled at the reference to his old school. His father had been proud that his son had attended Birmingham's first comprehensive. But Len's next words troubled his son. 'Dad, Dad,' said Eddie to the screen, shaking his head ruefully. 'Don't you remember? We didn't walk in together on my first day at Longbridge. You were on nights.' Nonetheless, his father looked cheerful, happily showing off his collection of strike memorabilia.

The film cut to Len pottering around the garden, stopping to pose for the camera beside the shed. Eddie grinned at this, but as Len turned away to walk back up the garden path, Eddie saw that his father had aged. Len's back was hunched, his gait laboured and unsteady. The next clip, shot in the house, caused Eddie to grip his tablet hard. His father and his son were sitting on the sofa talking about Tel's engineering course at college. Eddie felt a rush of conflicted feelings as he contemplated his absence from the boy's life. Finally, the film showed Len sadly making a cup of tea and taking it across to sit in his threadbare armchair. No more than four or five minutes of film, yet it was so much to take in. His father was far more frail than Eddie had imagined, and plainly lonely, too. And the darker thought crossed his mind that the old man's memory was failing. As for Tel, the video was so different from the photographs he had seen. The boy seemed so much like he had been at that age that Eddie felt his heart might crack.

LINDSEY DAVIS

The Telemachus File

Ten years after the last sighting of the missing businessman and adventurer Odysseus, Midlands Today revisits this extraordinary case to see if there is any chance of resolving the mystery...

CLICK!

It may not have been a coincidence that Poseidon was on annual leave and not looking at his emails. He never made any secret of his impatience with the Odysseus situation. In his absence, the other professionals gathered for an interdisciplinary case conference.

Chairing, the normally relaxed Zeus grumbled about the Aegisthus Enquiry, which had certain parallels. 'Inevitably, the blame comes down on us professionals. The family were known to us. We can demonstrate due diligence over Aegisthus himself, who had been identified as dangerous. But what if a woman is willingly coerced even after the police warned her? Should we have foreseen that the son would then turn up at the house and end it all in a bloodbath?'

'Just have to stick to "No comment while it's *sub judice*",' Athene put in quickly. 'Now can we look again at the Odysseus file? There is now supposed to be a sighting of him living with a Ladyboy in the Far East, possibly under duress. If I can get agreement from you all, I would like to make Interpol enquiries.'

'It's Poseidon's department,' answered Mr Heaven. 'But

Odysseus was an inspiration in his day and a great Midlands benefactor. This is in the public interest. Let's put our heads together. If all the rest of us are agreed, I can't see Poseidon objecting.'

Athene answered gratefully, 'I want to renew diplomatic efforts to bring Odysseus home. In the interim, there's the son.'

'Quick recap?'

'His father left when he was new born. Possibly social services should have stepped in, but the mother seemed stable... Telemachus no longer needs supervision but I advise more counselling before he is cut loose. Someone must persuade him to take a stand. A hostile takeover group are targeting the family business, corporate raiders who are known as the Suitors. Telemachus won't need the Job Centre if the Ithaca Board resists that successfully, but he could lose everything if the Suitors break up the conglomerate. Maybe he should organise one last search for his missing father, or at least try to get definite news.'

Athene herself paid Telemachus a professional visit, though she went incognito to lessen the confrontation.

At the Odysseus home, a huge executive spread in a West Midlands gated community, the Suitors were lolling by the heated swimming pool, playing computer games on their laptops and eating takeaway meals they had ordered for themselves on the family account. Amongst them lurked Telemachus, an introspective loner, dreaming of how his father might return and see off these spongers. He alone noticed the newcomer, standing ignored on the well-landscaped drive. He went up, shook hands and offered the old Black Country greeting, 'Come in; sit down; what can I get you to eat and drink?'

He led the stranger indoors to a luxury leisure area, wanting privacy to ask questions about his absent father. But the Suitors came swaggering in, flopping on the leather furniture and playing music on the wraparound sound system. Uniformed caterers appeared with trays of food and drinks. The suitors began bopping amongst the designer sofas.

Telemachus leaned in to the stranger and whispered confidentially, 'I apologise. This gang of reprobates are living scot-free in the home of a man whose body lies unburied in some distant land or rolling in the sea. They'd scoot away fast enough if he showed his face, but he's gone. I have to face it; he is never coming back.' He pulled himself together. 'Never mind that; tell me about yourself.'

Athene made up a tale, pretending a past friendship with Telemachus' grandfather. 'He and I go way back – but I gather he has isolated himself on an organic farm and never takes the train into New Street nowadays? Honestly, I came because I heard a whisper the Big Fellow was home. I mean your Dad . I won't accept that he is dead. He must have been captured by pirates living off ransoms, or stranded on a desert island. Even if he had had a satellite phone, the batteries would be finished by now. Surely we'd know if he had died. We would feel it. Until there is definite evidence, you have to have hope.'

Gazing at the boy, the stranger then said, 'So you are Odysseus' son! I used to see him all the time, though it must be twenty years back, not since he first set off to that war zone on his tragic relief mission. You're just like him.'

'My mother says so,' replied Telemachus. 'It's a wise child that knows his own father without a DNA test. But if I am, my old man is the unluckiest ever.'

'Well, with those parents, there's hope for you,' said the stranger. 'But what the heck is going on here, lad? It looks like a celebrity wedding at a stately home – are you offering open house twenty-four/seven? Who are these people, all behaving like louts in a TV docudrama?'

'Good question!' Telemachus soberly replied. 'This used to be a happy home, but that was before my father vanished. Knowing nothing of his fate, we cannot find closure. No funeral, no memorial service, and we can't bring ourselves to declare him dead formally... But there's worse now, because every slap-happy entrepreneur in the Midlands want to move in. This lot are all trying to date my mother, though she hates the thought of making a new commitment. While she's toying with online matchmakers, hiding behind a fake profile, my so-called 'uncles' keep hanging around, eyeing up father's business empire, choosing their own steaks to throw on the barbeque without a by-your-leave. I'm quite sure they are hoping to edge me out of the business soon in some deadly take-over.'

'That's terrible!' sympathised the stranger. 'It's certainly high time your father reappeared and turfed the blighters out. He was handy when I knew him. What a lad!... There's no way out, Telemachus. You're not a kid any more. It's up to you now. If your mother wants another man, let her. But you should call a Board Meeting, let everyone know you are joining the business, and that your first project is a new investigation, using air and sea rescue services with modern search techniques, and looking in new areas. You must aim to establish whether your father is alive and coming home. If he is, you can last out a little longer like this. But if he's gone, you should put up a plaque in his memory, then move on. Your mother too. Get a grip boy.'

'I am finding this really helpful. I'd like you to mentor me,' Telemachus pleaded.

'I'm afraid I don't have the time at the moment. Anyway, you don't need me. Your CV has too many blanks, but you have skills. You are going a long way. So think on!'

'I really appreciate everything you have said. How can I thank you?'

'Some other time,' said Athene, as she slipped away.

But she had achieved her object. She left young Telemachus inspired. He was even more concerned for his missing father than before, but felt the change in himself, fired up with new courage.

Now the Suitors were listening to 'The Long and Winding Road', drooling away to it in drunken karaoke style, a long chain of them swaying, arms around each other's shoulders as in Greek dancing. It brought his mother from her room; with her came her two girlfriends, teetering on six-inch heels, each wielding a big glass of chardonnay. As backup for Penelope they were rubbish, but perhaps helped somewhat in a loud gathering of men, all half-seas-over.

'Don't play that!' snapped the woman of the house, pulling the plug on them. 'Aren't there plenty of miserable ballads you could listen to without upsetting me with that one? Have a drink by all means; listen to something that doesn't make me well up in tears. But please! Spare me a song that always reminds me how I have lost my wonderful husband.'

'Cool it, Mum.' Telemachus surprised her. 'To them it's just another Golden Oldie they can sway along to mindlessly. They're not thinking. Don't get in a strop; it will only cause strife. Go back in your room and leave it to me. I'm going to sort this lot out.'

Penelope was taken aback. Not normally one to follow orders, she nevertheless left him to it. She was delighted to see her son coming out of his shell – and pleased to have an ally at last in her difficult situation. Even so, she could not avoid a pang of anxiety, a premonition of the empty nest.

If Telemachus was growing up, she would be more alone than ever. Penelope could never stop missing the husband she had loved, her soul-mate, and that night as so many times before, she cried herself to sleep.

The Suitors burst into uproar, each openly lusting after Penelope who was still good-looking. But Telemachus showed nous, even though he called them to order. 'Fellows, if you want to win over my mother, don't disrespect us! A little less racket, if you please. Let's eat up and drink up, enjoying the moment. I have an announcement: Tomorrow I am summoning the company board to an Extraordinary General Meeting. There is a recession. We need to retrench and restructure. I'll be announcing a shake-up where, inevitably, people who aren't expecting it will face redundancy.'

They were amazed. Antinous exclaimed, 'You may be your father's nominated heir, but you are not Chairman of the Board yet!'

'I would not turn the post down,' Telemachus rebuked him. 'There are plenty of fine executives in Ithaca Inc. and its great parent company, Achaea Holdings; some are more experienced than others. With Odysseus dead, I become the major shareholder and, if offered, I don't intend to refuse.'

'The Board must decide,' Eurymachus sneered, adding insincerely, 'Nobody wants to rob you of what is legitimately yours... But my dear Telemachus, who was that you were hobnobbing with earlier? It looked like a consultant of some kind. We all know what that means in business. Has the position changed at all, regarding your father's disappearance? Are there new rumours?'

'Just an old friend of Dad's, mithering about the old days. I have stopped listening to rumours, whatever their source,' Telemachus said. 'And I don't take any notice of the psychics my mother calls in. I don't need a crackpot medium to tell me. My father isn't coming back.'

Accepting his bluff, the Suitors shamelessly hung on past midnight, still partying, until they called for taxis and tottered off to their own houses. Telemachus had gone to his room upstairs, a lonely boy's retreat, where for a long time he searched the internet obsessively, trying to find answers. Eventually Eurycleia, a household fixture who had been his childhood nanny, came in and persuaded him to turn off the computer. Even after she hung up his clothes and tiptoed away, Telemachus lay awake under the duvet, turning over many thoughts in his mind and planning action.

At first light his alarm woke him. For once the young man responded, reviving himself with a hot shower then dressing in an elegant designer suit, with handmade shirt, gold cufflinks and limited-edition tie, before being chauffeured in a limousine to the city centre offices of Ithaca Inc. These were all stone cladding and tinted windows, in a sidestreet close to St Philip's Square: discreet new wealth in the old bank quarter. Close by lay the popular nightclubs and casinos in Broad Street, including those owned by Ithaca.

Ithaca had been founded by Odysseus, building on the Greek restaurant chain of his father Laertes – which still thrived, its latest venture being the Dardanelles, where the Trojan Horse special mezes were legendary. (Real horsemeat, some cynics said.)

In his time Odysseus had been an aggressive businessman, creating his empire with resourcefulness for which he was still remembered, a man both wily and inventive. Part now of the conglomerate Achaea, Ithaca still retained a large degree of operational independence. Its decreased prominence these days was only due to the mysterious absence of its founder. Even so, for twenty years it had been successfully steered behind-the-scenes by his wife Penelope. She gave an impression of vagueness and apparently spent her days buying craft kits from TV shopping channels, yet she was highly intelligent and a superb organiser. She had fended off takeover bids for two decades and showed little sign of flagging.

As all eyes around the boardroom table fell on the handsome Telemachus, the elderly Aegyptius called them to order. He had lost a son, gunned down in the Cyclops massacre, and had never got over it. 'We have not had an Extraordinary Board Meeting since Odysseus left. Who has requested one and why? Has he heard that the missing have returned, or is it some other matter of public concern? Good for him, in any case!'

Reassured by this auspicious start, Telemachus took the floor.

'Sir, I called for the meeting. There is no news. This is to address the double-pronged attack on the business and myself. Not only have I lost my father, who supported me as much as he did all of you. Now a bunch of pestering menaces are besieging my mother, trying to make her commit to one of them and to get their hands on her shares. They have already affected our profit margins and nearly ruined the company GDP. Some of you are on protected contracts and may not be worried, but I say we all need to consider the future viability of Ithaca Inc.'

At first they were stunned.

Finally, Antinous took it upon himself to issue a rebuttal. 'Don't blame the Board, Telemachus. It's your own scheming mother who has for too long been ducking out of decisions. She writes private emails, making promises to individuals, then deletes them instead of coming good. And for three or four years she has set up a smokescreen of a 'consultation process' that she says must be completed before we can move forward. Her consultants are going round in circles and never produce their report, while Penelope slyly encourages them. Luckily a whistle-blower brought it to our attention. So long as Penelope maintains her misguided attitude, corporate raiders will keep Ithaca in their sights.'

'I cannot go head-to-head against my mother,' replied the wise young executive. 'There would be a public outcry and I won't do it.'

Instead, figures were produced to show that the conglomerate was under pressure. Halitherses said his piece: 'I am not an accountant, but I can read a balance sheet. I am for caution. I've always said Odysseus is resourceful and he will return. Believe me, it could be any day now.'

Eurymachus was having none of it. He told the old man it was time he resigned from the Board, then he ordered Telemachus to over-rule his mother, so she would approve the Suitors' takeover.

Telemachus wisely stayed calm and referred that back

to the Board. Meanwhile he sought agreement to his plan for one last search for his missing father, asking for funds. 'If I hear that he is alive and returning, we can weather one more year. But if he is gone, yes it is time to issue a death notice and reassign his holdings – including my mother's.'

Mentor, the old ally to whom Odysseus had given power of attorney, took the other directors to task for sitting silent. The meeting broke up. Telemachus would be assigned an expedition fund, though in reality, no one thought the young man capable of bringing it off.

He himself sought solitude, wandering along to Brasshouse Passage and down to the canal, its still waters dark as wine among the moored narrow boats. He texted Athene, who met him in person. She bolstered him with more inspiring words: 'You have your father's wits; you are neither a fool nor a coward. Don't dwell on the Suitors and their plots. Start putting together your expedition. I can help bring in friends and equipment.'

Telemachus had a heavy heart, as he set off for home to make ready. He found the Suitors grilling meats on the barbeque, but shook off their false offers of friendship. 'You have robbed me blind, while I was too young to understand, but your day of reckoning will come – and it will be bloody. I'm off to consult the others who went on my father's mission with him.'

They responded with insults and even threats, but he left them and began making his arrangements. Eurycleia, the fond carer who had always been his rock, helped him pack. She begged him not to go, but to stay and lead a safe life unlike his father, and prevent the Suitors causing havoc the minute he was gone.

'When the going's tough, the tough get going. I have to do this. Don't tell Mum until I'm gone, so she can't stop me. No need to worry her until it's unavoidable...'

The Suitors were comatose, zonked out after Happy Hour. As darkness fell, Athene led Telemachus from the family home, bringing him to the eager comrades who would share his mission. The young man took command as they loaded up their transports with provisions, seek-and-find equipment, telecommunications gadgets and the latest navigation aids. His young team were talented and eager; even the weather forecast was promising. The well-packed vehicles moved off in a disciplined train. Mission Daughter of Zeus had commenced, the first brave step for Telemachus towards the time when he would stand alongside Odysseus, father and son, putting all to rights.

So Telemachus began his search and his journey into manhood, as he travelled away all that night and into the dawn.

ELISABETH CHARIS

So Far from Home

Blood had been spilt and somebody had to be punished.

It was hardly a flow though; not exactly blood splattered over the classroom walls; no bags had been set on fire, no body parts broken and no flashing ambulance lights disturbed the lessons. There was barely an ebb even – a small dot of scarlet on some folded toilet roll, but there had been excited clashes and serious threats.

Dee had sat in his office afterwards soothing the boy through his vibrant rage.

'You've got to think about your future,' he'd said, the timbre of his voice too empty: he knew the world the boy was in. 'You need to stay out of trouble. If you get excluded, it's harder.'

'I don't care,' the boy said, sitting and putting his foot on the chair in front of him, 'This school is bullshit. It's all bullshit.' He waved his swollen hand over the clutter and lifted his chin to the world and sky outside the window.

'You have the chance to do something better,' Dee said.
'Like what?'

'Something secure. Don't you care about your family?' But there was no point trying to reason. The boy had his crew and too much to prove.

Dee had appealed to the head for lenience: he knew an expulsion would only push the boy further into trouble but the head had cast his decision and it couldn't be questioned. When it came to it, it *was* bullshit. They didn't care about the best interests of the kids. It was about appearances.

Afterwards, Dee stood on the steps watching the boy swing his injured limp down the school drive like a medal. His phone sounded as the boy reached the main road and the black, gliding arc of a seagull slid across the white sky reflected in the screen. The mewing of the flock marked the post break-time looting of empty crisp packets and scraps of sandwich. Two texts, one from Tina, his line manager, asking for an incident report and one from his wife asking him to pick up shopping.

'Parents evening. Back late,' he texted his wife and turned off his phone.

'What about your son?' she had asked the last time he was held up. He hardly was anymore. He went out so little now his friends had stopped calling.

These days, wakeful nights had him shivering on the edge of the bed, studying the dark frame of the looming wardrobe while his wife brought the crying child between them. Such sleeplessness was a torment of memories and endless calculations, balancing the spending habits from his previous life with his *respectable* salary. And, for what seemed like hours, his wife's pathetic pleading to the child.

'Just put him in his room. Ignore him. He'll soon toughen up,' he'd suggested once. He didn't dare suggest such a thing again.

Last night, waking to piss, he deserted bed to wander about the house. His father, rising to pray, found him, sitting on the step watching a bright vein break into the dark sky.

'This time is about the mother,' his father said and patted his head. 'Your time will come later.'

Parents' evening was all sweaty handshakes and fixed smiles. Dee greeted parents at the door in person, guided them to the teachers, placated, translated, reassured. As assistant head, Tina was too busy to rescue him from the emotional cornering of the fighting boy's mother, but Kayla, wandering round checking on colleagues, pushed a cup of tea into his hands.

'Drink', she said, 'You need a break.'

'I'm surprised to see you here,' he said, 'I didn't think artists would have to come to parents' evening.'

'I don't, but I said I would support the art department. It's nice that you thought about me though.'

'I didn't. I mean–'

'It's alright. I'm just teasing,' she said, smiling.

'You coming for a drink?' she asked him later as they stacked tables.

He looked at the small crowd of his colleagues gathered by reception. He wouldn't normally.

'I don't drink'.

'I don't drink really,' she said, unwinding her light hair, 'You never come out with us.'

Half an hour later, the usual people sat in the beer garden at The Village; support staff, a few young teachers and Kayla. Henry, one of the senior management team, was there too, bringing a stiff politeness to the group until he emptied the dregs of his wine and got up to leave.

'See you all tomorrow,' Henry boomed as he left. He gave a mock salute to the group and turned to Kayla, 'Bye Kayla. You in tomorrow?'

'Yes and again on Friday,' she said and Henry left. 'Oh he's just being friendly,' she said afterward to the raised eyebrows, and 'he's not my type.'

Someone passed round a joint and the mood changed. As he smoked, Dee sunk into the warm wood of the bench and let the day and chatter wash over him. The sounds of birds in the bushes around the edge of the garden trilled a dark syrup of his thoughts. Everything beyond his inner world blurred except for the regular breaking of Kayla's bright laugh. She caught him watching her and smiled. A haze of gold flies fretted around her head.

Later, some of them walked through the balmy evening to The Bulls Head for the reggae night. Dee walked with them.

'Come on, Dee. Lets go dancing,' Kayla called when he stopped at the bus stop.

'I should go home,' he said looking at his phone.

'Is someone waiting up for you?'

'Probably not'.

As they waited at the bar, Kayla touched his shoulder, 'You wanna come out back for a smoke,' she took his hand and led him to the garden. 'You had a bad day?' She asked, looking at him, her pink tongue wetting the line of glue on a Rizla paper.

'Day?' he asked. She laughed that laugh again.

'Oh dear. I heard about whatshisname. He'll be okay,' she said, lighting the joint and sucking a red crackle to the tip.

'It's not him I'm worried about,' Dee said.

'Oh right. Maybe you need to chill out,' she said, and passed him the joint.

Inside the club, the bass in his body coursed like fear. His sense of self spread out like ripples. A tide of people came in through the door, pressing him onto the dance floor. He began to move, gently, tension seeping in shivers from his skin. In front of him, Kayla's eyes were closed but her body was loose. When she opened her eyes and looked at him, he was pulled by her, anchored. Everyone else blurred to a blaze of face and limb. The music made him spin, chopping and turning, churning round; his body drowning in the waves of dark and light. He gasped at clarity as it spun, shining above the music. Her movements became the only thing. First, like the soft tide pulling but soon she was reckless. Her body crashed around him and he tumbled, helpless, alive.

Later, there were flashes of hot moments, walking, groping down the road, leaning into large front garden trees, against walls, grasping, her mouth soothing his desperation, the stairs then wall of her hall. Her hands pulling him out of himself and into her face, her body.

All day on Tuesday his throat was glass. He got hard thinking about her dancing. He sat twice in the toilet waiting for his body to follow his resolve.

In the corridors her face gave nothing away, but she held his gaze once for a moment when no one was watching. In snatches amid the clatter of tea-making at break they agreed it shouldn't have happened, that they should talk. She couldn't do that day or the next. He tried to capture the memory of her smell but could only think of the salt on her skin.

Friday they met at the allotments near the school and walked through the park to her flat, two arms' length apart. They talked about the week, the fighting boy's exclusion, the overrunning parent's evening. He complained about his workload, the hollow rhetoric of the head's speeches, how unappreciated he was, how tied.

He watched her pale face carefully through sideways glances. She watched the ducks and coots settle around the lake, touched the hanging leaves of the great trees arching over them as if they were her friends. She stopped and pointed at the far off flecks of gull swirling like specks of dust catching light.
'I never do understand why they come here,' she said.

'They have guaranteed food,' he said. 'We give them rich pickings.'

'But to be so far from the freedom of the sea–'.

At her flat, he sat in the kitchen drinking tea. She stood and leant against the sink, one hand holding her elbow, one hand swishing the teabag around her mug and looking at him. Sun warmed the basil and thyme on the windowsill and filled the air with sweetness.

When there was nothing else to say instead, he got up to leave. They stood again in the hall by the kitchen.

'It shouldn't have happened,' he said, grabbing her arm.

'I know,' she said, and leant back against the wall. She didn't pull her arm away. He didn't let go.

'Don't worry,' she said and let her head fall back. Her

arm dropped and he let his hand fall along it, stroking her skin for the briefest moment, then grasping again as she leant forward. Then his mouth was on her, and his hands.

'We should stop,' she said.

'I can't.'

This time he was as lucid as the darts of sun on the draining board. This time he steered them through the hot swell of her bed as the afternoon dwindled.

That whole half term his head was filled with their after-school liaisons. He became familiar with the synchronised trails the ducks chugged through the murky blossom on the lake in the park en route to her flat. He began to know the trees. He rehearsed answers in case he bumped into students; *I've just come to clear my head; I'm just getting some exercise; Shouldn't you be doing your homework?* Tense cups of tea progressed quickly to fast, loose sweat and rushed, guilty showers. His work began to slip.

'We are concerned about you, Dee,' Tina said when he arrived at her office for their weekly meeting one day.

'We?'

'The leadership team and I.' Dee swore quietly and sat down on a chair in front of the only window. It looked along the corridor. 'Henry asked me to speak to you about the lack of follow-up on some of the incidents lately.'

'Henry? I thought you were in charge of pastoral care. Why would he get involved?'

'Some of the teachers are concerned. There have been some violent incidents lately and you haven't stepped in.'

Dee sighed. 'I'm just not sure what the point is. I know these kids. I know their world.'

'That's why they need you, Dee. You can relate. You are their chance. You can lead them.'

'I don't know,' he said and picked the corner of one of her bright wall displays. 'I'm just not sure about a lot of things–' he wanted to tell her about this woman, their shared workmate, *his* woman. He talked instead about his wife.

'I'm thinking of leaving her,' he said finally.

It wasn't as if he hadn't tried. Yesterday he went home earlier than usual, on a wave of guilt. But his wife busied herself till bedtime. When he climbed around the familiar curve of her and kissed her neck, yeasty and sweet with coconut, she'd pushed him away, waking their son with the sharpness of it.

Tina shuffled papers and looked at the clock.

'You have to do what's right for you,' she said. It was easy for her. Her world was different. When he tried to talk of his sinking faith she said, 'There are many ways to God.'

He thought of that when Kayla's pale arm and breast were resting on his torso later. She picked at the damp, black hair of his chest. They lay in silence. The afternoon sun lapped through the slatted blinds and clattered erratically against the tall window frames. There was so much space here, so much quiet and light. Over the shushing of traffic from the main road, Dee could hear pigeons coo above the distorted peal of an ice cream van.

'Here comes the smack van,' Kayla said building a joint, but the waves of light rolling through the trees made a soft joke of her words.

He tensed his neck to watch as she got up to walk around the room. Her naked pacing and sometimes dancing would stir the threads of incense into swirls around her. Sometimes she would tear the curling, brown leaves of the enormous lily and screw them into the soil. Sometimes she would just pick through the stacks of vinyl and spines of books. Her clothes, she kept elsewhere and he never saw her change.

'Why do you live this way?' he asked. 'You don't have to.'

'What way?'

'This way. Why don't you get some nice things?'

'I like my things,' she said slowly and knelt to run a finger down his middle. He kissed her, hard again. It went on like this. His stays each day reached further towards evening and one day, at the end of term when the weeks ahead threatened, he didn't go home at all, just sent a text, 'Don't wait up. See you tomorrow,' and turned off his phone.

Tomorrow, the air at home was stiff with fried chillies. The cousins were visiting, a curse-blessing: there was no space for questions. The children ran around on a holiday high. His wife babbled, clattered, cooked. His son was everywhere.

The cousins left late and he went to his own bed. His son was in his cot for once. His wife was there facing away from him, her breathing grasped and stuttered, her dark hair a shadow between them. He searched for sky through the window but from his bed could only see bare brick and a clean corner of newly fitted PVC frame. When his wife's breathing slowed he got up, packed a bag and left.

But after each fervent night of the summer with Kayla he woke heavy. Whole days got lost under stacks of empty takeaway containers. Mornings turned over his beached thoughts and sunk. The afternoons he spent perched on the wicker chair by the window and watched the rolling skies. Lines of poplar from the park waved their heads in greeting but offered no answers.

One afternoon, as Dee watched the shadow of gulls cross the pavement towards the park, she had a visitor. Dee saw him crossing the road to Kayla's and recognised Henry's wide swagger immediately.

'I'm popping out,' she said, 'back in a bit'.

On her return, Kayla began cleaning.

Gathering his clothes, he left the bedroom to press her.

'What's going on?' he asked.

'I'm going away, to a festival,' she said, gathering up a pile of empty takeaway containers and stuffing them into a bin liner.

'What? When?'

'Tomorrow.'

'Oh.'

'Yeah. Should be fun. You want some tea?' she asked, filling the kettle.

'What will I do?'

'Maybe you should go home. See your son. You want tea? I need to get packed.'

That night they fell still and silent into sleep until the dawn spilled a rose light into her bedroom.

'Let yourself out when you're ready,' he heard her say, 'Drop the key downstairs.' Then she kissed him softly on his temple, stroked a hand across his hair and was gone.

After seven years she had probably moved on. She was not the sort of person to stay fixed, but Dee still found himself guiding his family to the part of the park nearest her flat. It was safe now though, he wouldn't be caught this time. That, and he had run out of reasons not to take them to the visiting fairground.

He still knew the trees. Birds, children and dogs still fussed about the lake, but she wasn't there. Long after the children's dinner-time he conceded that they should go home. In the car park a shout brought him back to the present.

'Arright, Sir' a young man driving an black Audi lifted his sunglasses to speak to Dee. It was the fighting boy: older, muscular, with a gold tooth now.

'You're doing alright then.' Dee said putting his hand on the car.

'What's it do?'

'Nought to sixty in about nine seconds. Good beard, sir' the boy said pointing to Dee's face. 'How you doing?'

'You know, surviving.' Dee smiled at him.

'I heard you disappeared.'

'Well yeah. Moved on. I run a school in Alum Rock now.'

'Your own school? Going up in the world, Sir.'

Two of Dee's children hung off him pulling at his trousers and cuffs. He sent them to the car with his wife.

'You still hear about the staff then?'

'My little cousin goes there.'

'So who's still there?'

'A lot of people left after you.'

'What about that art support? What was her name? Miss-'

'Oh yeah, that fit one? She had a baby. I int seen her since.'

'When?'

'Dunno. Five or six years maybe.' The boy's phone rang.

'Gotta deal with some shit, sir. Laters.'

The growl of the engine almost covered the roll of thunder from the blackening horizon. A seagull swooped in with a hankering cry and landed in front of Dee on the shimmering tarmac to pick at a soggy ice-cream cone.

'Bloody seagulls,' he said to nobody.

In this city, there was no space anywhere, except the sky.

KIT DE WAAL

Adrift at The Athena

Ulysses Tate walks uphill in early evening light, the air tainted with city fug, heavy with unspilt water. He's developed a shuffling gait over the last few miles in the soupy August heat and his overcoat is killing him. He stops and takes it off at the corner of Reddings Lane and Stratford Road, leans against the glass of a shop window and wipes his sleeve across his face. He has a long way yet to go. He sits on the concrete step of The Athena Launderette, its door is wedged open and it reeks of clean. Down the middle aisle, between banks of washers and dryers, there is a single wooden bench, wide as a raft floating on mock marble tiles. The strip lighting hums overhead and the whole place invites him in.

He closes the door behind him and walks straight to the back. There's a small office, padlocked and next to it, the big industrial machines, as tall as the man himself. He shucks his overcoat over his shoulders and takes everything off, his old boots, his jeans, his blue shirt, his underpants, his socks. He puts his coat back on and bundles everything else into a machine. He buys a small box of powder from a dispenser and fills the plastic chute to the top. He feeds in a few coins and hears the water rush through the pipes, watches his clothes turn sodden black. Five items. Everything he has.

He pushes the bench against the dryers and settles his boots on his lap. He stretches his neck left and right, crosses his bare feet at the ankle and leans back against the cool metal. He listens to the slosh and slop, the rhythmic agitation of his £3.75

wash, the churning of the drum and somewhere nearby a woman singing. He shuffles into comfort and closes his eyes.

After a while, at the edge of his consciousness he hears an alarm and a door banging but he keeps his eyes shut and stays in his dream. He's remembering a baby's bath and his arms in the soapy water, splashing, getting wet, the baby laughing, the water tickling his skin. His dreams pull him under sometimes, leave him frantic, gasping for air but he's found, over the years, a way to surf the in-between time, skim over the water and stay afloat. He's learnt to half-sleep through screams and fights, retching and masturbatory grunts, broken sobs, oaths and beatings, but the sound of a girl's voice brings him up, back to life.

They stand over him, two of them, arms folded.

'They're bad shoes, man. 80's shoes,' says one.

'They're boots, Sasha. Or boats. Yellow suede boats.'

'Nubuck.'

'Old buck, you mean.'

'He's drunk,' says the first.

'He's mashed,' adds the other.

'He's a tramp.'

'Yeah, a tramp. Or a vagrant.'

'Is it vagrant? Or vagabond?'

'Whatever. He's naked, that's all I know.'

'Yeah, a flasher.'

'Or pervert.'

'That's what I'm thinking.'

He draws his coat about him and looks down at his feet in a pool of warm water. He lifts them up on to the bench.

'Cover yourself, man,' says one of the girls and they draw back giggling covering their eyes.

He sees her then, twisting a mop in a bucket, a young woman, older, taller.

'You two go on,' she says over her shoulder 'I'll catch you up.'

'No, Nicci, man,' they say.

'You can't.'

'Leave it, Nicci. Do it later.'

'Everyone will be there, Nicci.'

'I can't,' says the woman. 'It's everywhere. Go on without me.'

The two girls shake their heads, pretty heads held at an angle, their eyebrows plucked into accusing arches, red-painted downturned lips, each sheathed in the skin of a dress, red for one, orange for the other.

'I don't like leaving you, Nicci, man. He could be anyone.'

'Worse than that, Sasha. He could be someone. Know what I mean?'

The woman with the mop stops but doesn't turn.

'Are you someone?' she asks.

'No,' he replies. 'No-one.'

'See,' she says and resumes her mopping. 'Go on. I'll catch you up.'

They hold hands, trip with dainty steps through the soapy water.

'Don't be long, Nicci.'

'Uncle won't like it if you're late.'

They turn the sign from 'Open' to 'Closed' and drop the latch on the front door.

The woman keeps her back to him and he watches her move. She's slow and easy in her green rubber clogs and bare brown legs. Her silver jacket shimmies as she moves, her black dress waves at the hem as she dances the mop across the tiles. He can see her neck and wisps of hair that curl against it, he can see the side of her cheek, her strong hands but he cannot see her face. She makes shapes with the mop on the floor and she's quiet, concentrating as though she's writing a poem, a love letter.

'Suppose that's my fault,' he says.

Her head moves a little in reply.

43

'Maybe I didn't close the door properly,' he adds, 'or something got trapped.'

'That would be my guess.'

'I didn't see anyone when I came in.'

'You don't get much business on a Saturday night. I live in the flat above. I just came down to lock up.'

She writes, moves the bucket along with the mop, writes again.

'Was it you singing?' he asks.

'I don't sing.'

'Maybe I was dreaming.'

'You were talking.'

'Must have been rubbish. I didn't say anything did I?'

Her head moves again as an answer but still she doesn't turn. She is so close he could reach out and touch her, bring her round to face him but he doesn't move.

'You're not dressed for it,' he says drying his feet with the hem of his coat. 'Should have got your mates to pitch in.'

'They're my nieces,' she answers.

'Pretty girls.'

She rings the mop, twists it dry and picks up the bucket. She turns to him at last, smiles and as she walks away she shouts.

'Young enough to be your daughters, I should think.'

He watches her unlock the office and go inside. He sees a light come on, hears her moving about. She comes back carrying a folded white sheet.

'So, everything went in. Pants? Socks?' she says.

'Yes.'

'Because?'

'They had a smell.'

'Of?'

'Somewhere I'd like to forget.'

She nods.

'And your coat,' she says touching him on the shoulder.

'It doesn't smell?'

'Yeah, but ….'

He folds his coat around his chest. He's lost weight since he last wore it. And he has lost, almost, the memory of that last time and his woman's face as he left. His last sight of her. His fingers splay across his chest where he feels the loss. He must go home.

'Take it off,' she says and hands him the white sheet. 'Put this on. I won't look.'

She turns from him, opens the door of the washing machine, pushes his few things to the back and slams it shut. As he winds the sheet about him, she stacks the plastic laundry baskets, throws empty soap powder boxes into the bin near the front door. She flicks a switch and one of the strip lights splutters and dies.

He throws the end of the sheet over his shoulder, holds out his arms.

'What do you think?'

She picks up his coat, puts it to her nose.

'I think they all smell the same. Heat, sweat and cigarettes,' she says. 'Which one?'

He doesn't speak. She holds the coat towards him. 'Empty the pockets,' she says.

He takes out his bus ticket, a pack of chewing gum and the little wooden horse. She opens the door of a dryer and throws the coat inside. She pours a handful of soap powder into the palm of her hand and sprinkles it over the coat. She turns the dial to 'Cold', puts a coin in the slot and turns it on.

'A trick,' she says and sits down next to him.

'How do you know?' he asks.

'We clean anything, 'she said, 'coats, curtains, carpets. Wedding dresses are our speciality. Didn't you see the sign outside? Women dream about their wedding dress. They want to be a princess for a day, the whole fairytale, the handsome warrior fighting dragons, rescuing her from the tower and then the happy ever after. But first,' she holds up a finger, 'the dress.

Anyway, after the wedding, you've got the wine stain, the chocolate, the sauce, the lipstick, the soup. Those two girls, my nieces, make them white again. Between this place and the drycleaners next door, we make dreams come true. Sometimes a handful of soap powder is all it needs. If we can clean a wedding dress, we can clean anything.'

'I didn't mean the trick,' he says.

'I know.'

She walks to the office again at the back of the launderette, straight, long strides in her plastic shoes, her thin dress skimming her skin, it would be damp to his touch in the hot night, sweaty from her work. She leans in and takes out high heeled sandals, black and silver straps. She eases each foot in, twisting her heel, pointing her toe.

'That's better,' she says.

'You didn't answer my question.'

She wipes a cloth along the top of the washing machines.

'I have five brothers,' she begins, 'One has a chip shop, one has a garage, one has a rich wife. Two I see every fortnight at the Visiting Centre. The same smell on them and afterwards on me. I queue up, show my passport, take my shoes off, get frisked. You know the routine.'

She polishes the doors and the chrome handles and speaks quickly as she worked.

'You on your way home?'

'Something like that, yeah.'

'Is she waiting?'

'Who?'

'You were talking in your sleep.'

'Sort of. Maybe. Hope so.'

'What were you in for?'

'You're not supposed to ask.'

'I know.'

'I lost my bearings. Got into fights. Got paid for it sometimes. Stupid.'

She turned quickly and caught him.

'You're staring,' she says.

'I've been away a long time.'

'I wouldn't if I were you. My Dad wouldn't like it. Nor my brothers.'

'They're not here,' he says quietly. 'There's just you and me.'

She folds the cloth in half and sits next to him on the bench. He can smell her over the detergent, light and fresh. Her flat above would smell the same, her pillow, her bed.

'I used to play in this launderette,' he says

'Yeah?'

'It was called 'Speedy Clean' back in the day. Used to mess about with my mates. Smoked in that doorway there. Broke in and slept on this bench when I was a kid.'

'Is that when you bought them boots?'

'Funny,' he says. 'A comedian.'

'Comedienne. Female.'

'I'm trying not to think about that. Don't want to get told off again, do I? Or get roughed up by your Dad.'

'You've done some roughing up yourself by the look of you.'

That same smile.

He feels the rough hairs on his chin, the bristles on his shaved head, the scar that runs across his cheek, the matching one on his throat. He has lines on his forehead but his body is firm, fatless.

She crosses her legs and smoothes her dress over her lap. She looks at her watch.

'Where are you supposed to be,' he asks. 'You don't wear that dress for mopping floors.'

'An engagement party.'

'Yours.'

She shrugs.

'You didn't mention him,' he says.

'When?'

'In the list of people that wouldn't like me looking at you.'

'He must have slipped my mind.'

Click.

The washing machine begins to thrum and whirr. His few clothes spin into a blue blur against the drum. It will be over soon and he will have to be on his way.

'They'll need drying,' she says. 'Ten minutes ...'

The rain comes suddenly, violent and beats against the window. A boy and girl, hand in hand, huddle in the door. The boy whips off his jacket off and slides it over the girl's shoulders. She smiles up at him, touches his face and as they kiss he draws her in, cradles her in his arms. It's a film star's kiss, tender and sweet, the boy's hand on her cheek, hers on his neck.

Ulysses and Nicci sit and watch.

'Youth,' he says.

'Love,' she whispers.

Then the kiss turns into something else. The young couple begin twisting into each other, writhing. The boy pushes his girlfriend backwards and she flattens against the window, her wet hair spreading across the glass like black ink. The boy snakes his hand up her blouse. Ulysses imagines its path. The long narrow valley of her spine, the soft curve under her arm, the pulpy, bloom of her breast, the bud of her nipple. He can see the side of Nicci's face, the blood flooding her cheeks, her lips open and her breath coming quick.

'It gets you like that sometimes,' he says quietly, 'like something from above. You're not in control.'

'I know.'

'Don't look,' he says, 'leave them to it.'

He touches her then, turns her face to his. He moves a twist of hair, brushes her cheek with his fingers and she leans to meet his touch. They are quiet together, with the music of the spin cycle keening higher and higher until the dial clicks again and his socks and pants, his jeans and shirt, fall in a small heap and come to rest.

'If I wasn't on my way home…' he says.

'I know.'

'I've been away too long.'

She nods.

'Who's the toy for?'

He picks up the little wooden horse.

'It took me years, this did. Smoked a lot of cigarettes and started collecting the evidence. I made some duds but this one came out alright. 224 matchsticks. Sanded them smooth, you can still see the lines. See? I burned two circles in the wood for the eyes, here. Varnished it. Sanded it. Varnished it again. Then got some hair from the guy on the bunk below. Told him I needed his ponytail.'

'That's not true,' she says but she's smiling again.

She gets up, takes his coat out of the dryer and throws his clothes inside. Then she stands looking at him, her arms folded.

'Come on,' she says. 'Your turn.'

He follows her to the back of the shop, shuffling in his white robes. In the little office she moves her chair aside and puts soap and a towel on the side of the sink. She holds her hands out for the sheet. He hesitates. She unwinds him and he turns slowly but as the sheet peels away he stops, looks away, shakes his head.

'Turn around,' she says as she fills the sink.

He feels her hands slippery on his skin, the water tickles, runs down his back. The soap is her smell, sharp and fresh. She kneads the hard muscles of his shoulders, the sinews on his neck. She hums while she works as though he isn't there, naked almost, the folds of sheet drooping around his hips. He's heard her song before. It has the lilt and flow of a lullaby and Ulysses knows that he could sleep to it, properly sleep, lose himself for a lifetime. If he turned around, he could rest his head on her chest and she would cradle him, cover him, rock him like a baby and he could lie back, cast off, let go.

'It's alright,' she says. 'Ssssh.'

She covers his back with a towel and holds him from behind until he becomes still.

'I'll go and check on your clothes,' she says.

He blows all the breath from his lungs, steadies himself on the sink. He is on his way home. He has to go home this time. He plunges his hands into the hot water, washes his arms, his pits, feels the warm rivulets trickle over his chest, dribble into his groin. He makes a lather and soaps his belly and his balls, up between his cheeks and the top of his legs, down between his toes, splashing himself with water all the time, rinsing and wiping and rinsing again. He refills the sink, smooths his palms over his face and the back of his neck, his shaven scalp, his ears and as he bends to rinse the soap from his eyes he hears her outside the door.

She knocks and he ties the towel around his waist.

'Come in.'

'Here,' she says and puts the pile of clothes on the table, 'all clean and dry.'

His jeans have shrunk to fit and his socks are soft. He buttons his shirt, takes his time. Takes a deep breath again, wonders how to say goodbye.

She stands with the keys in her hand.

'You look different with your clothes on,' she says. She folds his collar down, brushes some powder from his coat.

She leans into the office, flicks the light switch, turns the key in the padlock. He should go now. He walks to the front door.

'Wait,' she says.

With that same smile, she puts the little horse in his pocket.

'You never told me your name,' she says.

'Ulysses Tate.'

'Nausicaa,' she says and holds her hand up, 'Don't ask. It's a long story.'

She turns out the light. He is standing close to her in the warm, lilac light of The Athena Launderette. Sparkling beads of rain on the glass make patterns on her face and catch the light in her eyes. She links his arm.

'Come on, Mr. Tate. I've got my Dad's car outside. I'll take you home.'

'You're a good woman,' he says, 'you know that, don't you?'

She moves her head a little as a reply. He sees the curls again on her neck. Stops himself from moving them, touching her skin.

CHARLIE HILL

Odysseus weeps, as the bard at the Phaeacian games tells the story of the Trojan horse...

... blimey it's hot. where am I again? let's see. that was Park Hill, we've had the church, there's the Prince – looking good as usual – so this must be...ah yes. Chantry. the very same. carpet of cherry blossom, frondy beds, perfumed billows of flowers. Nice House Road if you will and of course you will and how did i get here, if anyone asks? oh, the usual, you know me. passing through. carried by a breeze, blown by the wind, born on the whims of the gods of wine and chat, looking for heaven knows what...well. texted anyway. 'there's a barbie on. open house type-thing. pop by, I'm sure you'll be welcome.' I'll bet. bound to be someone there who knows of me. got to be close to a fixture at this sort of thing by now, as i drift from gathering to gathering, a little bit legendary, a little bit mysterious. it's a dirty job and all that. could do with it too – a few tots, maybe a few stories – way i've been since last week, since that party on Cotton Lane. thought i was losing it there, a couple of times. head music. most unlike me, most odd. oh well. onwards, as ever. up the drive, front door's open, in i go. aha! so it's **his** do. I've heard tell of him, of his get togethers. he's Moseley royalty, he is. excellent. i can certainly live with that and...oh my. it **is** a Nice House. let's see. oak floored hall, big stairs, feature vase, or is that an urn? telly in there, kitchen through there. into the back room – nice fireplace – smell of cooking meat – pork, maybe – coming in through the French windows. aah! French windows – simple, timeless – why mess with the classics? – and now a patio. moss-aged brickwork. pastel blue wall. honeysuckle/ivy trellis, ooh, that's nice, a ceramic mosaic, goddess/nymph-type thing, mirrors in her hair, mischief in her eyes... there's the barbie. wooden table of food, one, two Greek salads, bowls of olives, hummus, and what's that? aha, baba ganoush. quite a crowd an' all, no surprise there. power milling holding court, bit of the old woffwoff; typically Mose by the looks. professional class or thereabouts. the modestly great and relatively good: teachers, academics, arts administrators, probably the odd theatre designer, session musician, internet summat. the vibe sunday-boho: understated statement shirts, an occasional beard, the odd pair of – ouch – inadvisable shorts. teens and kids too, detached, or running about in a boutique-festival style. let's see: Cassandra? that figures. Drew? hmm. Megan but of course. more wafts of meat. bi-ig lawn, fire pit. tinkling: glasses on glasses, laughter, keyboards, the music rocksteady, i recognise this one – Jackie Mittoo – a little bit out there but safe enough – comfortingly familiar, reassuringly exotic – very Moseley, very Nice House Road. so. where do I start? glass of wine and back into the front room i think. telly was on, showing the Olympics. might settle the nerves, dispel the jitters – yup, anxious again, head's not quite right – why is that? – help me to get my bearings before i dive in... phew, it's cooler in here. and – bloody hell – maler than outside, if that's possible. surfeit of Team GB shirts. poor chat, though there's no surprise there. typical sports fan shortage of wit – 'Did you know the Olympics started in Much Wenlock?' says a fella in leather sandals. and then, of course, a tautness of nearly pros, in the corner, once removed from the hoi polloi. genuine athletes. clean shaven, less booze, thin muscular. climbers i'll bet, or runners or cyclists. L'Etape, no doubt – oh yeah there it is. wait til they clock me – a little bit lairy, a little bit hairy – i'll be fair game. someone's bound to come the billy big bollocks, *though this is Nice House Road so it'll be on the sly.ahh,* he's the fella: *him there, gesturing at the telly in a triathlon tee.* I Do It For The Pain. *please, please tell me you're not trying to impress me with that – swig of wine – oh here we go – what's that mate?* 'Do you follow athletics, then?' *i knew it. challenge disguised as polite enquiry. ok, ok, you asked for it (and thank you, goddess whoever you are...):* 'Not any more. I used to. When I was a kid, I was area champion at the javelin. And there was none of this aerodynamic rubbish they throw these days, I can tell you. Lead mate, made out of lead they were...' *do you see, mate?* '...so yeah. But then – cut a long story short – I went abroad for a couple of years, did a bit of travelling in the Med. Hitching rides on cargo ships and ferries and the like, dodging civil wars and revolutions...' *and yeah, you might look impressed,* '...which takes it out of your body in the end. Not that I'm unfit – you just pick up a different sort of fitness. Do you know what I mean?...' *so there you have it. you* **did** *ask. but then that's me, that's what i do these days, when i'm on my game at least – another slurp. i tell stories. and do you know why, mate? (been thinking about this.) because anyone can go charging about the place, doing stuff. triathlon-ing – though that's the least of it – and the rest. i mean i've done my share of that. i've made hell and merry on my travels, seen palaces and kings, i've shadow-wrestled with politics and monsters and love. but it isn't enough. you've got to tell the world about it too. because that's where you're alive, in the telling, in your stories, in the way you choose to edit the stuff you do. in fictions – anecdotal, honed – in rhetoric, self deprecation, the piss-take and front, in observations and asides, in apercus and pith and one-liners and wit. in 'have you heard?' and 'you'll never guess what', in stories that get you out of bother or into bed, that help you sleep at night, or give you confidence or a finger up your arsehole. in chat that makes you laugh or gives you peace of mind. i'm wiser in my stories, wiser, funnier, more enduring, more heroic. better too, better at everything i'm known for, better at sports, better at love, better at* *drinking and fighting, at telling stories or work – whatever that is – better at being a shit or swearing. or, come to think of it, worse. i mean that's the thing, it depends how it plays. so. how* **did** *that chat play, with the rest of the room? am i on my game? let's see. quick scan, bit of eye contact from that bunch over there – not too much, some down the nose; lots of averted gazes. you don't fool me. i see that interest, those smirks – sandal man, i'm looking at you – you've been listening alright, all of you, of course you have. because everyone listens to someone like me. because you might be alive in your own stories, but you're alive in other people's too: you're him he's talking about or her, the hero or heroine or villain or dick; you'd have done that slightly differently – shake head – or that just the same – affirmative nod... any road. that's enough of that – rub face (still not right, jitters unassuaged) another drop – blimey wine's gone – it's time to move on, leave this lot to their sports and games. looks like the fella in the sandals is coming too. maybe i've got myself another follower. hmm. not sure what i think about that just now. oh well. pffff. onwards, as ever. into the back room. and what do we have here? small group of people in front of the mirror by the fireplace, more typical Moseley woffwoff. holiday chat by the sounds: beardy bloke taking the piss, her in the maxi dress doing herself down and wait for it... yeah, there it is: the obligatory sat nav gag.... should i dive in there, give them the benefit of my chat? i could tell them the story about wild camping on Paxos, some of the lads falling foul of the local brew, the lass with the glint in her eye; or the one about when we were threatened by that gangster, crippled fella lived up in the mountains... face it, it's all quality stuff. that's why i'm in demand. then again – blimey that's some frown – do you know what? i'm not sure i'm in the mood for this after all. for any of it. bit discombobulated to tell the truth, bit all over the shop; pulse's skittering, breathing's rushed – is that heat or wine or am i losing it again? i don't know but i need to sort this out, whatever it is. into the garden i reckon, listen to some tunes – the music's still good; spot of Toots – get some air, that* *might help. through the French windows – mind the step – that wasn't very cool –and outside... ah. patio's full. sea of people, haze of voices. very close. very sweaty. no air after all. hotter than before, if that's possible. oh well, i'm here now. deep breath – in through the nose, out through the mouth – quick refill and in i go for a (hopefully restorative) mingle. let's see. what's the chat like? blimey that's pedestrian, even for Nice House Road. all marinade recipe this, Instagram that, book group the other. wireless providers. that or nostalgia, the old ones reworked, retold –* 'do you remember Chloe? Chloe ran away with Tom'; 'what about Penny?' 'Penny with the beret?'; 'No, that was Dennis. Dennis goes glamping' – *oh this is no good, no good whatsoever. it's more than pedestrian actually, it's stultifying. oppressive. and it ain't helping my head. neither's he, as it goes. sandals man. holding court by the halloumi kebabs. he's looking rather smug all of a sudden, a little supercilious. it's as if he's orchestrating the conversation, but there's more to it than that. ever since he heard my chat, he's been trying to catch my eye. almost as if he wants me to take the floor again, tell a few more stories, like i'm some sort of entertainment. I don't think so, mate, really i don't. i mean where do you get off with that? who do you think you are? who do you think i am? and now – oh great, it gets better – now he's trying to liven things up by giving everyone the benefit of his own chat.* 'I know this one! It's an old Trojan Records number. Takes me right back, I can tell you, to summers and being young...' *here we go* '...the world was bigger back then, do you know what I mean?...' *oh really? do tell* '...but that didn't stop us from wanting to see it. That's right! By any means necessary! One chap I remember had a crazy idea about setting off in the footsteps of...' *hang on* '...yeah, he was from round here as it happens...' *hang on a minute. is that... is that me he's talking about? i mean i remember that too, well almost at least* '...last anyone heard of him he was in jail on Gozo...' *it is! that's me he's on about! – well sort of at least – Jesus Christ! talk about kicking a man when he's down. is this what it's come to? is this* all i am round here? someone to be trotted out like Tom or Dennis or Chloe whenever the chat gets too Dennis or Chloe or Tom? is this all i am? existing – enslaved – in fragments, anecdotes, apercus, one-liners, sweaty above the perfumed gardens of Mose – a javelin champion travelling the Med, dodging wars and revolutions, a chap from round here, with a crazy idea, last seen in a jail on Gozo – in fictions, part-truths, evasions distortions. in stories. edited? bullshat more like. reworked? retold? regurgitated more like, by gatherings of Moseley royalty, by professional Nice House Roaders living vicariously up or down, living through me in so much woffwoff – comfortingly familiar, reassuringly exotic – like over-chewed youth or barely palatable thirty-plus regret, like the cud of a goat, the bullshat cud – yeah that's right – the bullshat cud of a goat – did I ever tell you about that goat I saw on the back of that mule? it was three in the morning blah de fuckitty blah. pfffffffffff. fffppbbbbbb. rub face. i mean don't get me wrong. we're all made-up. we're all stories. that's where we're alive, in the stories we tell ourselves and other people, in all this stuff that happens once or doesn't and then is told and told again until it does; we become it – i become it – 'that's epic, mate! you're a legend!' as the son of that fella said to me the other day. but i'll tell you the difference, i'll tell you the difference, it's this, this is the difference: I've told too many stories. it's all i am. i've told so many stories i've lost myself, i'm alive in other people's chat but nowhere else and, and... whoah. whoaaah! there's that thing again – from Cotton Lane – fu-uck – this is too much, the pressure's almost physical, it's all closed in and my brain's gone, just gone, disintegrated fragmented, i'm in pieces, thoughts diffusing – floating away, evaporating in the air around my head – Jesus – squeeze eyes tight shut blink – need to sit down – but where? – deckchair by the barbie, collapse, head in hands – pretend it's ok – 'smoke's in my eyes' and now – what's this? – the tears – huhhhhhuhuh – a snivel a heave and i'm gone, my Christ i'm gone... hhhhffffffffffhhhhhh... right. right. enough. come on son, take a minute, get a grip of yourself.

through the nose, through the mouth. so i've gone, have i? well then, i need to come back. because whatever i've become and wherever i am, this is me and there's nothing i can do about it: i can't stop telling stories, because it's all i am and all there is. so i've got to keep going. gathering the pieces, the fragments, putting them together. making new stories, telling more stories. i'll become whole again – sometime, soon – i have to. in a minute: at next week's gathering, a do a month from now, a year or two on; eventually, if only in passing. and until then? well, another deep breath, let's see. stand up. allow myself a smile (Christ. of sorts...). more wine – of course – a fumbled olive, some rice from an opened vine leaf. who's this? oh great the host – what's that? 'what do i do?' 'that's a good question...' *rub face, keep going* '...this and that, you know? Actually, you'll never guess what...' *and onwards, onwards. ever onwards...*

PAUL McDONALD

Who Are Ya?

Keith

The fight they had in Kiev following England's Euro 2012 loss to Italy never made the papers. Ordinarily, this would have disappointed Keith Keating: as leader of the Walsall supporters firm, Trojan Horse, he enjoyed making an impact; today he just wanted to get home.

They'd arranged it online and a dozen of Keith's lads met twenty Italian Ultras in a quiet spot on the banks of the Dnieper River. It was midnight and they couldn't see who was who in the dark so Keith ended up half-braining his mate Clifton with a bottle of Lvivske Pilsner. Fortunately, the police appeared before Keith knocked Clifton's IQ down to a single figure, and they spent the night in a holding cell. The following morning, as the rosy-coloured dawn illuminated the iron grill of the window, Keith addressed the five Trojan Horse members who'd failed to outpace the coppers: Matty, Wayne, Stevo, Colossal John, and, with his left eye swollen like a bastard, Clifton.

'Lads,' he said, stepping onto a bench in order to command the room, 'it's the usual drill. They'll have to charge us or release us; and remember to be polite at all costs.'

Wayne groaned, 'One of those useless twatting Italians ripped the collar off my Versace!'

Keith assured him that he, like the rest of the lads, still looked the dog's bollocks, and Wayne perked up. They respected Keith. He'd led Trojan Horse for 10 years and proved himself in combat countless times. They'd met all-comers together, arranging rucks all over the Midlands, England, and the world: West Brom's Section Five, Wolverhampton's Yam Yam Army, Birmingham City's Zulus. They'd fought them all and never disgraced themselves. Keith's wife Penny was forever asking him why a forty-two-year-old estate agent continued to behave like a hooligan and his answer was always the same: it was his only way of commanding respect.

'Do you think they'll press charges?' asked Colossal John. He was balanced on a metal toilet in the corner of the cell with his strides round his ankles; he looked like Shrek crapping in a Coke can.

'I doubt it John. Think about it: we didn't clobber any coppers and, to be fair, no one likes Italians.'

The lads murmured their assent and Keith rolled up the sleeve of his blood-speckled Armani shirt to give the traditional salute: a raised fist revealing his gang-name tattooed along his inner forearm: Odysseus. Keith's firm cheered and raised their fists in response.

'Who are we?' Keith bawled with his fist still raised.

'Trojan Horse!' they shouted, and Keith stepped down from the bench.

It thrilled him when the lads responded in that way: he was proud to be a leader and loved his life with the firm. He could never resist taunting other firms with their battle cry, ensuring they knew their name, and his own. But that morning Keith didn't feel quite the frisson of pleasure he usually felt, and this worried him. He'd enjoyed the ruck well enough – he disliked Italians even more than the Welsh, Scots, Irish, French, Germans, Danes, Swedes, Norwegians, and whatever you call people from Greenland – but another conviction could mean a long stretch inside, the loss of his job, and possibly Penny too. Keith knew it was wrong to dwell on these things, but as the guards approached his cell door he couldn't help wishing he was back in Walsall.

Kyrylo

Kyrylo Kyryloyshyn didn't get where he was in the Ukrainian Militsiya by being a nice guy. He didn't get there as a result of looks, intellect, or crackerjack acuity either: he had a face like a monkey's arse, an IQ of 86, and a glass eye. No, Kyrylo reached his position in the Ukrainian Militsiya because his dad got him the job.

Today Kyrylo wasn't in a good mood. Interrogating English football hooligans was so far beneath his status that he laughed out loud when he received the request. That was usually a job for the uniformed police, but infuriatingly he was the only person available who could speak English. He'd been at home breakfasting on lamb cutlets when the call arrived and it irritated him beyond expression. Reluctantly he donned his double-breasted work suit and size 17 loafers. Kyrylo owned an extensive collection of cosmetic glass eyes that depicted a host of moods from perky to pitiless, and he spent more time than usual selecting an appropriate one for the occasion: eventually he opted for his 'jaded martyr eye' with its drowsy, shrunken pupil framed by pinkish white.

At the station Kyrylo's mood wasn't improved by the fact that the Englishmen were clearly nobodies. Or at least the first five he interrogated were. The one who Kyrylo saved till last, and who smiled confidently across the desk at him, had the bearing of a somebody; indeed, he had the bearing of somebody Kyrylo didn't like. Kyrylo didn't like that he was handsome, he didn't like that he seemed clever, and he didn't like that he had two good eyes. Kyrylo half-wished he could replace his 'jaded martyr eye' with his 'brainy bastard eye' – its crystal clarity and incisive pupil might help suggest that he wasn't a man to be trifled with. But it was too late.

'Name?' barked Kyrylo, holding Keith's passport open at the photograph.

'Otis Dodgewell,' said Keith, 'but you can call me Otis.'

Kyrylo leaned back in his chair and narrowed his good eye. 'You come to Ukraine to cause trouble Otis Dodgewell? You think you are a big man, somebody who can run riot on our streets?'

'No sir,' said Keith, 'I'm really just a nobody who wants to go home.'

Kyrylo was flattered to be called sir, a term the Englishman employed throughout his questioning. Seldom were football hooligans so polite. It wasn't long before Kyrylo was persuaded by the bloke with hair like hyacinth clusters. He was willing to believe that he was indeed 'a nobody' caught up in the swirl of bother; certainly Kyrylo saw how that might happen, and he knew how annoying Italians could be. He hated Italians; he hated the English too, of course, but at least they knew how to stand up to the Argentinians, who he hated almost as much as Russians, Hungarians, Bulgarians, Estonians, Latvians, Algerians and Greeks.

Kyrylo informed the uniformed underlings that Mr Otis Dodgewell wasn't worth the paperwork, and may as well be set loose. He then told them that he was off home to finish his cutlets and if anyone had an issue with that they should take it up with his dad.

Keith

On the subway back to the hotel the recently-freed members of Trojan Horse were jubilant, not least Keith. The huge one-eyed copper who'd questioned them was a very dim bulb and he'd swallowed Keith's patter sweet as a treacle tart. He swallowed his false passport too. For five years now, Keith had been required to surrender his real passport to the police during any overseas tournament in which England was involved. The falsie set him back four grand but it was worth every penny. It was always good to get one over on a copper:

he'd stitched the one-eyed freak up a treat, even nicking the pen off his desk right from under his bulbous Ukrainian bugle. That had been daring, reckless even, but it delighted him that he'd had the brass bollocks to do it.

Despite the fact that they were in a crowded subway carriage Keith couldn't resist celebrating. Standing on the shifting seat he steadied himself with a leather hand-loop and revealed his Odysseus tattoo.

'Who are we?' he cried, giving the fist salute.

'Trojan Horse!' shouted his mates, and Keith's shoulders swelled.

By the time they arrived at their hotel it was midday and most of their firm had checked out, heading for the Black Sea beaches. The five who'd been with Keith overnight would follow tomorrow, while Keith himself, aware he'd had a lucky escape, wanted home. Back in his room he booked himself on the 23.45 flight to Heathrow, despite it costing him an extra four thousand Ukranian hryvnia. If he took the Heathrow Express into London and the fast train from Euston to Birmingham he'd be in Walsall before noon tomorrow. When he tried to phone Penny to tell her his plan she didn't answer, and he was in the process of texting instead when his mobile rang. It was Wayne.

'Oi Oi Oi!!!' said Wayne.

'Who are we?' said Keith

'Trojan Horse!' shouted Wayne, who then told him that he and the other lads were keen to sink a few beers down Khreschatyk Street. 'Let's go mental!' he said.

Keith thought about it. Part of him knew it was a mistake; part of him always knew, but that didn't stop the letters of his tattoo tingling irresistibly.

Kyrylo

Kyrylo Kyryloyshyn didn't get to be leader of the Kiev-based firm, Cyclops, simply because he had one eye. Although appropriate, his monocular status was a huge disadvantage. The reduction in stereopsis and peripheral vision meant a distinct lack of hand-eye coordination and profound clumsiness. Every time he threw a punch he was as likely to hit one of his own mates as a combatant. No, Kyrylo got to be leader of Cyclops because his dad made them elect him.

After interrogating the Englishmen Kyrylo had taken the subway home. Even from the opposite end of the carriage he was able to spot the so-called 'Mr Nobody' standing on a seat and crowing. Kyrylo was enraged. This cheeky bastard thought he was a big man who could shit on Kyrylo's patch! He thought he was a genius somebody like Hitler or Columbo! How could Kyrylo not have realised? He had been duped because he'd let himself be flattered; he'd been drunk, his dad might've said, on his own self-importance.

The Englishman made a fool of Kyrylo and now he was in trouble. Who did he think he was?

The fiercely patriotic Ukrainian saw little distinction between his role in law enforcement and his role with the firm, and he definitely hadn't forgiven England for beating Ukraine one nil in the group stages of Euro 2012. He'd been to England several times with Cyclops and fought and won. He loathed the English who, come to think of it, were far worse than Italians. He was going to give them the kicking of their lives! He was going crunch their sorry heads together!

Ordinarily Cyclops arranged fights with firms via their Facebook pages or bulletin boards, but Kyrylo decided to take the Englishmen by surprise. He followed them back to their hotel at a discreet distance, wagering a billion hryvnia that from there they'd head for the bars of Khreschatyk Street to celebrate their release. The English were so predictable.

Kyrylo tracked Trojan Horse to a bar called Hades and then made some phone calls. With his apartment nearby he had ample time to change out of his work suit, don a XXXL Ralph Lauren hoodie, and a pair of Calvin Klein jeans. Replacing his 'jaded martyr eye' with his crimson 'combat eye,' Kyrylo headed back to the bar.

Keith

By 6pm the lads were already raucous. Wayne was annoying a couple of local women by comparing Kiev unfavourably to Bloxwich, and Colossal John was attempting to teach a group of bewildered Spaniards the words to 'Vindaloo.' Matty and Stevo had pinned a huge Cross of St George along one wall of the bar and were toasting it with tearful renditions of the 70s football classic 'Back Home.'

Keith tried several more times to reach Penny on his mobile but she wasn't picking up, and he was about to try her again when he saw them. He could spot a rival firm through a pair of lead goggles and when Cyclops arrived he knew they were in for bother. They were difficult to miss. Some had their jackets zipped-up to their noses and wore baseball caps with the peaks pulled down; others sported hoodies with scarves wrapped around the lower half of their faces. They weren't as well-dressed as British firms, except for one large bastard in Ralph Lauren. The firm made straight for the England flag, cutting a swathe through customers.

Trojan Horse engaged the enemy immediately and ferociously: he saw Wayne neatly dispatch one with a right-hander, and Stevo take out another with a roundhouse kick to the slats. As leader Keith felt obliged to go for the big bastard, who seemed to be scanning the room looking for someone to clobber.

'Oi tosser,' said Keith, 'Who are Ya? Over here if you're

hard enough!'

The big bastard turned and advanced on Keith, taking a running swing at him. The Walsall man dodged it easily and the blow hit an elderly Ukrainian gentleman, knocking his spectacles across the room. Keith snap-kicked the big bastard in the bollocks but he hardly seemed to feel it and came again, throwing another punch; once more this missed Keith completely, hitting a hanging basket and creating a spray of soil and petals. Keith gave him a fierce jab to the jaw but the big bastard absorbed it, grabbed Keith by the lapels and pulled them face to face:

'Hello Mr Nobody!'

With his hoodie and scarf Keith hadn't recognised him, but eyes to eye he saw who he was dealing with. His thoughts ranged from panic to rage. He panicked at the idea of mixing it with a copper, but was enraged to be challenged. The one-eyed bastard seemed about to nut him so he had to act fast. It was Keith's fighter instinct that moved his hand to his pocket and the pen he'd nicked from the copper's desk that morning. In one swift movement he bought it up to the Ukrainian's good eye.

In the ruckus that followed Trojan Horse fought like lions. Within minutes they subdued the Ukrainian firm and made for the door victorious. Despite the obvious need for a rapid exit, however, Keith couldn't resist pausing to let everyone know who the Kiev firm had been bested by.

He raised his right fist with his tattoo exposed: 'Who are we?'

'Trojan Horse!' cried the lads, and Keith felt the familiar rush.

Five hours later Keith was thirty thousand feet above the wine dark sea, about to descend into England. He felt back to his old self again: a conquering hero returning to his woman's arms.

Kyrylo

It wasn't his position in the Ukrainian Militsiya that enabled Kyrylo Kyryloyshyn to exact revenge on Keith. The only things he was really known for among his colleagues in the Militsiya was cocking stuff up and behaving like a twat. No, Kyrylo was able to exact revenge on Keith because his dad did it for him.

Practically everyone in the bar on Khreschatyk Street had heard the English firm's battle cry, and saw Keith's tattoo. Odysseus aka Otis Dodgewell, aka Mr Nobody. Kyrylo's outraged dad was at his son's hospital bedside within the hour, and by midnight he had every police document ever written about Walsall's Trojan Horse downloaded onto his laptop. With the connection between Keith, Odysseus and Otis Dodgewell established, he simply made a phone call.

How Kyrylo's dad was able to bring so much influence to bear on everyone in Kiev, Ukraine, Eastern Europe and the world was a mystery even to Kyrylo. His dad had always been an enigma: he couldn't even fathom what he did for a living, and ultimately gave up trying. Was he a businessman, a politician, a gangster, or a god? It often seemed he was the latter: feared and respected by all who thought they knew him.

Keith

It was an exciting time in Winson Green Prison. As a special privilege the inmates were allowed to forgo lights-out and watch England's 2014 World Cup game against Italy on the communal TV. It had been two years since Keith saw those two do battle in Kiev, but it felt like twenty.

He still wasn't sure what happened. When he was arrested at Heathrow the police knew everything about him, as if they'd been tipped off. They charged him with travelling on a false passport and, given his previous convictions, heaved numerous volumes of the book at him. Never reaching Walsall,

Keith was held on remand until his trial and then sent down for a three-year stretch. This was a particular ordeal because he shared a cell with a bull-muscled giant called Kalypso Kadogo, a man who curled his eyelashes and referred to Keith as his 'prison wife'.

Most upsetting was that Penny never visited. She wrote to him occasionally promising to stay faithful but claimed she couldn't bear to see him in jail. Keith was convinced she was having an affair. The Trojan Horse lads who visited him were cagey, but when pressed they alluded darkly to potential suitors. It was agony: how long would his reputation continue to keep them at bay? Penny and Walsall were so close, but so distant.

The final whistle sounded and Keith sighed: England had lost to Italy again. He needed to steel himself and remind himself who he was: he felt like a nobody now, but in less than a year he would be somebody once more: Odysseus, leader of Trojan Horse. He would command Penny's respect, and his own: his tattoo tingled at the prospect of being back in control of his destiny. As Keith returned to his cell he felt a little more positive, unaware that in an exclusive district of Kiev a god was making a phone call.

RICHARD HOUSE

Underworld

Buzz slips the razor into the front pocket of his backpack before he sets out. Checks that he has his passport.

Six men gather at the restaurant and there's a competitive air about them. The restaurant sponsors a local school and at the bottom of the menu runs an invitation asking English-speaking tourists to visit. You can borrow the teacher's bicycle to return to your hotel. They make the same sour joke about the bike and the teacher and Buzz watches the doorway knowing he'll forget this place, these people, as soon as he leaves. In forty-nine hours he'll be back in Bournville. The new arrival, his replacement, sits close, rubbing arms and legs. He wants facts, advice, has the same ideas everyone arrives with, and Buzz doesn't want to spend any time setting him straight. He doesn't want to learn the man's name (Ron, Rod, Robbie, Robin?) because he isn't going to use it. Advice? All you need to remember – however screwed up this experience becomes, and it will get screwed up – is that the five-point programme produces measurable results. 1. Medication. 2. Land clearance. 3. Education. 4. Assistance (which includes sponsorship for artificial limbs, vaccinations, and any retraining that isn't covered in education), and 5. Special Assistance. 5 is the item you need to be careful with. Where possible, avoid item No. 5. Make sure you remember that. Otherwise, just be clear that whatever you're doing fits into one of the aforementioned categories and you can't go wrong. The other volunteers add their own provisions. Don't take personal photos while working. Don't wander off established pathways. Document all shrapnel.

Don't tug at weeds and plants along the pathways, those things have roots, you never know what they're wrapped around. Take your doxycycline. Drink bottled water. Don't sleep with Buzz, ha ha ha (if you do, double-up on the doxycycline). Don't take it personal when someone dies, you'll wear yourself out. Buzz, a hardened volunteer, knows this last fact to be true.

They call this *collecting the dead*.

The newbie asks where they come from (Bremen, Iowa City, Belfast, Atlanta, Birmingham), and looks about the table a little shy, a little awed, as if he is seated with minor gods. The truth is they burn with their failures. Buzz especially. Buzz, who didn't like the earlier joke, hasn't had sex for, what, six months now, tells himself *whatever*. He'd sleep with this man (Ron, Rod, Robbie, Robin?) if the offer came up. A one night, final, no harm done. He wants to be in love, just a little, before he leaves. He wants to tell this man simple facts which have nothing to do with war. One, *the chairs are heavy because they're made of hardwood.* Two, *the colours people paint their houses have no practical use.* Three, *when we said don't volunteer for Special Assistance we were serious. Don't.*

At the end of the evening, Buzz takes the gifts, shakes their hands, promises he'll do his last duty at the hospital. With more goodbyes running through his head (goodbye Laos, goodbye Xieng Khouang, goodbye Phonsavan, goodbye Ricky's Café, goodbye table, chairs) he mounts his bicycle and disappears up the broad unlit street where the curb falls into gravel, broken glass, grit and dust.

As the flight comes into Vientiane he closes his eyes. He doesn't want to see the Mekong.

The luggage came first. Messages from the dead. A small valise spinning flat and quick. A blue suitcase tipped at an angle, caught in the flow and taken by a faster stream. Tied plastic bags, also spinning. Loose oranges in troubled brown water.

After the suitcases, clothes, stretches of material, a long scarf, sandals (soles up), a hairbrush, many water bottles, brought undamaged through the rapids to the islets, to the bushy banks, the wood quays, the rows of tethered boats. Three larger bobbing cardboard boxes stamped with a blue cross recognisable from the shore. Then a scattering of fist-sized, white boxes marked DP1024 (these, being held in the hull came to the surface only after the boat had fully capsized). Some of these reached Vietnam, Sa Doc and Ben Tre.

In Birmingham he's known as Andrew, or Andy, not Buzz.

He can't stomach the idea of going home, and dreads that last leg, the taxi from the station. He comes through customs in a hurry, heads directly to the train. His backpack on his shoulder, his head down, as if speed means intention. Once the plane broke under the cloud the grey and the green were painfully recognisable. Returning home was a fact.

At New Street he doesn't recognise the station. He decides not to take the train to Bournville, because he doesn't want to see the canal. The train rides level with it. Up from the platform he isn't sure about his direction. He'd promised to call and maybe there will be a meal ready. They will be watching TV. He knows this. He'll take his bags to his room. He'll sit with them, with the news or one of their programmes running a parallel commentary to their conversation. Their conversation won't begin to touch the years he has been away. Everything he has seen.

He takes a cab, tells the driver to take Pershore not Bristol Road, because this is the longer route. A new stadium at Edgbaston, and new flats. He tells the driver to stop when they come to Selly Oak. No. Take me to the station instead. For most of the drive he keeps his eyes shut.

Buzz hides his backpack in the bushes, the canal raised above allotments. He walks along the towpath, then sits alone, the canal a black and narrow trench. It's just water. Only water. Their first visit to Bournville when he was nine, a new arrival, and they came along this same stretch. The railway and the canal, side by side, something to see.

Night after night his dead come to him uninvited, blood-hungry. *Don't take it personal.* Easy advice, but no one warned him that new loss connects to old loss. Night after night, Robert, still blind, Terry who won't come forward until he's asked, and John who sits beside him on the bed, back-turned. Buzz wakes terrified. John was a practical joker, dead sixteen years he won't look good. One night, he knows it, John is going to turn around. He's grieved these men, long set them to rest – paper lanterns, vigils on beaches – but since the accident they've returned. Unsympathetic.

He's tired of thinking about them. Tired of going over the details. Sometimes he's awake and encounters elements, distillations, essential reductions. Someone who has a gesture that isn't theirs (Robert). A stranger in a market who knows a sequence of expressions (Terry), fine and detailed in execution. In a crowd, the back of a head (John), a certain tilt, a way of walking. Elements. Distillations. He'd rather forget them. More recently it's all about water. He does not want to go home. He wants to have nothing on his mind.

In Birmingham, he swears, he carries so much history. Some day he won't be able to move because of it. There won't be one fresh corner left.

He wants to listen to music – it keeps him occupied. He reaches into the backpack, front pocket, searches for headphones, draws out his hand and finds it wet, bloody. He's run his forefinger along the uncapped razor.

Buzz pinches his finger. Inspects. The cut is small, but there's no tissue, nothing to stop the bleeding. He stands, holds his hand over the canal, watches the blood collect at the fingertip and drop.

He calls them forward. One by one. First, Paul, Paul Weston. School friend. Bournville Paul. The reason he became a volunteer. Paul, twenty-six. Cystomegalovirus.

After Paul, Robert. After Robert, Gavin. After Gavin, Simon. Then James the carpenter. All back in '94. After James, Michael, Michael with lesions on his neck, scalp, and face. Buzz worked with Michael for eight months. That was the longest. After Michael, James, then Peter S, and Peter J who'd lost his brother the week before Buzz began caring for him. Peter J refused to eat. They took him to St. Thomas's and he didn't come back. That was the shortest at seven days. Peter J., Nigel, Andy, Mick, Joel. Buzz lists the men who were in his care. Handsome Joel who used to hum when he was thinking. Joel, Nathan, Andy. Of all of them only Nathan had family who would remember him now.

Buzz drips blood into the canal. He remembers these men. Calls them forward. Tells them, if you have something to say, please say it now. Let's end this. He releases a long breath, swears to himself, knows that nothing can be said, that this is all in any case a little silly. A vanity. He can't remember Terry's last name, Terry. Terry. Terry, god what was his last name? You forget how nasty it was. How medieval. The day-to-day attrition. How did anyone survive? When Terry went to hospital that final time, Buzz visited and read to him. They gave him injections right into his eye, but he still went blind. After Terry, Buzz moved abroad. Made the decision one morning, and that was it. Now he's back.

And here it comes, 5. Special Assistance, the accident on the Mekong. The women, tipped out of a boat, whose bodies were taken by the river from the placid flats to the rapids. Some caught midstream by branches, snagged hair, snagged clothes, all of these found face down, easily retrieved. Others less accessible, trapped in the upper cascade, jammed between rocks, some striped, some hooded by their clothes, some held under water, some, whose bodies were later dislodged, diverted the stream so that water rode their backs, fumed over their faces and made fountains of their mouths. Most of these remained in place for three or four days as they were inaccessible and too dangerous to reach. One, with a broken jaw, stuck upright and made to shiver and chatter. Others held upside down, underwater, some with terrible wounds struck after drowning, sides split open endlessly cleaned. The youngest girls, seven and fifteen, who, being smaller, had sat at the prow, were taken first and suffered terrible calamity in their struggles, tumbling from cascade to cascade, over half a mile, alive to the last, spun and broken, and carried, eventually, to calmer teal-green water. Not carried but thrust from Laos to Cambodia. All twenty-nine drowned.

They laid the bodies along the bank. Brought them to the centre, one by one, in boats. None of the volunteers had felt the disaster until the families began to arrive from Pakse.

Buzz does his best to remember them. He calls the women forward, bows his head, lets blood drop to the water, and tells them to go. Enough.

And finally, John. John Stores. John Stores who planned to go to America. Who wanted to escape. John. The first man he kissed. John Stores from Solihull. John Stores who didn't get to leave his country. John Stores. First love. Lost. Hardest felt.

Buzz doesn't know if this will work, but he can't carry them any more. The shades of these men. The shades of these women. He can't do it. If he's going to get home, he has to let them go.

DRAGAN TODOROVIC

Every Storm

In September, in Berlin, he finally finished the security software he was secretly working on for the better part of the last two years. It was a simple but elegant design. The programme would create a directory seemingly containing a large customer database. An intruder would encounter a set of serious defensive measures, built in layers. Each layer would eventually give in, feeding the attacker's vanity, until the gates would finally be crushed and the hacker would enter. The genius part was that, hidden among the data, were pieces of code that would self-execute once on the attacker's machine and start sending data about it to the security centre. The crucial element in the whole idea was the amount of resistance that the 'database' would put up. Too much and the attack would be aborted; too little and it would look suspicious.

By the end of the month the eight testers his company engaged for such situations, all experienced hackers from the Dark Cloud Triple6, confirmed that their computers were taken over by Circe. It was a huge success and he was proud of it.

He celebrates with his girlfriend Kika and a handful of their friends. The plan is to get a little something in the Turkish place up the street and then proceed to Ithaca, a nightclub in Friedrichshain whose owner Kika knew, but they underestimated the Turkish grill meister and they pig out. So they mostly celebrate by drinking sparkling water and bitters until they return to human shape.

Kika is an artist weaver and she gives him a present: a

poncho with an intricate masking pattern, black and grey and zigzag. She says it would make him invisible.

*

End of September and it's his best friend's birthday. He buys her a ticket and brings her to England for a long weekend in London and on Land's End. Penn has always liked dramatic landscapes. The weather is generous and they take long walks. On the edge of a cove they spot a small stone building that looks abandoned. The house stands like a single remaining tooth rotting away in the jaw of the cold cliff. He looks at the place and tries to imagine the people that once lived there. Why there? When someone goes that far from others, are they hurt or are they running away from the darkness inside them after hurting someone?

*

Kika laughs at him when he's naked. She says the composition is not quite right. She laughs, then gives her shiny, aromatic body to his contraption of bones and skin. He will leave her some day, but for now he keeps going back.

They attend the openings and premieres, book launches and conferences. Her friends are mostly pretentious and much less talented than they believe.

October is tightly woven. Kika's kilims are made of waves, every crest a golden thread. Those who walk on them have stigmata.

Too many gods for such a small world.

*

His company is a small operation, two other men and him. They are all computer security experts and their clients are banks, large businesses and even some states. Each project they do is expensive and that allows them to be relaxed.

Nevertheless, his summer is over and he needs to go back to Birmingham and take care of the sales of his latest invention.

In late November they rent a spacious house by the River Avon, outside of Stratford, and their invited guests arrive for the presentation. It is an international salad, a mix of bankers, government executives and experts. One of the London guests has brought his daughter with him. Her hair is the colour of wheat and her eyes the deepest shade of blue. The presentation goes well, but all he could remember the day after are the lips of Nusha Bulgakoff.

*

His apartment is in the city centre, on the old canal. There are two things he always wants close to wherever he lives: water and railroads. He has both here. The promise of distance.

*

Using something trivial as an excuse, he arranged for a meeting with Mr. Bulgakoff, hoping that Nusha might be his personal assistant or a trainee of her father, and that she would be there as well. She wasn't. Strangely disappointed, he returns to Birmingham, only to find a message from Nusha on his office system. Her father was interested in purchasing several licenses of Circe. Could they meet in two days to sign the papers and discuss the minutiae? Mr Bulgakoff was going to be out of the country, but Nusha's signature was deposited, too.

They meet on Brindleyplace, sign the papers and end up in his apartment, a few steps away.

*

I am entering your body as if it was a temple of a bellicose god. You've blinded the eye of my memories, and I won't remember anything but pain. With each wave you throw me back against the stone walls behind me. You carry me and you crush me. Every time we fuck I lose my name. Who am I? Who am I now, Nausikaa? Do you know me? Can you cure me? Will you bear me on this shore, love, will you give me life?

*

Sensing something, Kika arrives in Birmingham. They go for a lunch in an elegant Italian restaurant, then visit the Ikon Gallery. They climb up the stairs when entering, but take the lift out. The speakers, as always, play Creed's Work No. 409, a piece for choir and lift, but this time it has ominous undertones. As the voices descend from soprano to tenor to bass, he senses the metaphorical value of the sound.

They make love one last time, and he tells her about Nusha. She, for the first time, does not laugh at his body.

*

Early December. Penn calls to tell him that his father is not well. There is pain involved, and it won't go away. The early results arrive and they don't seem to be pointing in a good direction. Penn promises to investigate further. Two days later she calls him.

*

When he was 14 or 15, he dreamt of having enough money to build a village, and bring there all his friends so they could live together forever. Their girlfriends, their future children, their parents – all one tribe, one happy family till the end. But it didn't hold him for long. One of his friends moved to another town. A girl from the class transferred to another school. A boy hung himself. Only Penelope was always faithful to him.

And he realised that his dream was impossible, that

80

shedding friends is a signature of life. Every storm takes someone.

Like watching a ship from above: like being a god and watching a ship: the seas behind are oil and glass, the ocean ahead clouds and waves. The wake of your vessel sweet and strong, but ahead awaits a storm. And every storm takes someone. And every wake is a furrow from which no seeds grow.

*

He slowly moves his finger between his chin and her cheek, disentangling his beard from her hair. He sits on the edge of the bed. His back, lit only by the street lamp outside, looks like a drawing – curvy lines where folded sheets left their imprint, a couple of old scars, dark hairs shading his south. The tiny islands of the few moles, the Aegean Sea maybe. He is a man being drawn before her eyes.

'You've never mentioned your father.'

'I've never mentioned Lazar?'

'No.'

'He had a goldsmiths store, but he couldn't make jewellery, he just bought and sold gold. Then my mother inherited some vineyard, and Lazar sold his business. He worked the vineyard with his own hands. He turned out to be talented. His wines won some awards and he started earning. We started travelling. That money got me to England to study. When Mother was killed in an accident, he scaled down everything. I think he was depressed, but didn't want to talk about it. I offered him to come live with me, but he refused.'

'Is he old?'

'Sixty-three. Nothing.'

'What is he...'

'Metastasis. That's what Penn said.'

'Who's Penn?'

'My best friend, Penelope. She's like a sister to me.'

'Is she married?'

'No, why?'

She just waves her hand.

He stands up and walks to the window, opens it a little, and returns to bed. He finds her arm, pulls it closer and takes a smoke from her cigarette. The glow lights the tip of his narrow, serious nose. A man being drawn, piece by piece.

'And your mum? Tell me about her.'

'She was light, like a snowflake. When she died, we discovered she'd already taken care of everything: prepaid funeral, cemetery taxes, even deposit for the headstone. The priest asked for no contribution, so I presume she'd done that, too. Like a flake: fell on this glowing rock, quiet and beautiful, evaporated silently to where she came from. Time is powerless before people like her.'

She runs her fingers over his back, slowly, gently. She is a blind lover touching the smell, she is a painter fixing the charcoal, she is a mother, a shadow, a cloud.

'Why do I have a feeling that you're not coming back?' she says before she knows what she's saying. Once out, the words make her freeze.

He looks at her lips. Her hair. He looks at her lips. Says nothing. Touches the gentle skin under her eyes, as if trying to cover her circles, always slightly pigeon blue, turn them into shine.

'Why do you have that feeling?' he says.

'I don't know.'

'I'm not sure how long I will stay,' he says. 'Maybe that's why.'

A man, being erased, line by line, before her eyes.

*

All roads lead through brain, they are the convolutions in grey matter. Roads are memories and stories, roads create themselves when you travel on them.

A trip means learning. The destination is nothing but a measure of how much we expect to learn.

Three more hours to Köln.

Is this the road to home?

After all his journeys, he is not sure on which side of the road home stands – its beginning or its end. There were hotel rooms that he loved, and his own rented spaces he loathed.

He came to see home as a skin repository. Home is where you keep the old, dry, frozen you. Where you take a mirror but in it you only see your own abyss, the vortex of your memories. It's where you find a monster with six heads, several eyes, three rows of teeth staring back at you.

What he is now, he's not sure. He left because of the war, to avoid being conscripted. Lazar told him to flee, to just go. He ended up in England because he liked Black Sabbath. But there was no plan. Still there isn't. He started programming by incident, fell into it, became good, then became obsessed, and at some point a separate world enveloped him. It must be something like gravity, some magnetism created by the energy he'd put into it.

Then came his first successful project, a purpose-built shield for a bank. While installing that, he met his future two partners. Then there was another idea, and the money followed. He found himself in better hotels, with powerful people... and in a quiet world. That was the biggest difference between the times of have not and have: the level of noise. Money brings silence. And less gravity.

It's dangerous to remain in one place. He knew that early on. He had seen what happened to Penn, who did not move: loneliness, bitterness, in spite of what she said.

Just keep moving, just never let your feet sink into the asphalt below. Your enemies won't know where to find you, your head will be clear and fresh. You shed your friends along the way, true, you prune your telephone list, you cut off the dead branches, sweep out the dead leaves. Every storm takes someone. But you have to keep moving at all costs.

'I was about five or six when we moved to a new, much larger apartment. It was a spartan place for the first few months. We were too busy to notice the bare walls. The wine business was just starting to catch on.

Then Mama got a leaf cutting from Nada, a decorous old lady who lived three houses away. The leaf struggled to produce roots, and Mama started talking to it, to cheer it up, to make the flower forget its home yard and accept this window sill.

We found this odd, but Mama wasn't paying attention. She planted the leaf into a beautiful terracotta pot and the plant started growing and growing, cheered by Mama, until it became a beautiful blue violet, a crazy, exuberant bush that kept racing with itself to bloom again and again. Mama then got a white violet, then a whole family of violas followed. Soon, the pots filled the window sills and started spilling onto the dining table. Dad and I had to learn how much and when to water them, what temperature was preferred (there was one which lost colour from cold water), and what to tell them. They bloomed from kindness. Mama gave them names, joked with them, touched them. She started giving leaf cuttings to other women. Once even to a woman who'd given her one, but her plant had died. I caught Dad yelling at them a few times when Mama wasn't around, but it didn't seem to affect them. The plants just wanted attention. It created madness in the window. I've never seen such beautiful, perky group of flowers.

When Mama died, the flowers died. One by one, slowly. Dad gave the remaining pots away to the neighbours. In vain. A few months later Dad and I saw one of our old pots empty, with rotting stumps protruding from the dry soil.'

*

Angry. Angry. Angry.

*

How odd: a picture of a perfect life is unexpectedly easily shattered by something and suddenly all you see is an ugly backyard full of bricks and rusty nails. And you want to clean it up, to make it tidy, logical again. A pendulum that has stopped in its apogee is disturbing to watch.

In that new, ugly picture, order can be re-established only by starting anew, from the beginning, and in the beginning there was nothing. We often, maybe always, long for a clean plate, for that promising emptiness of our early years. Every nostalgia ever felt was for one's own youth, and youth means just that: having nothing but a promise.

Angry. Because nostalgia is soft and dreamy and silky... in poetry, in films, in music... and coming home is hard, rough, spiky, dangerous. Nostalgia is a lie. Nostalgia is middle-class garbage.

Another two hours, it seems.

*

He's always searching for himself when looking at the faces of those whom he's known a long time. Clocks don't wear out from measuring time, but faces do. Every minute shows.

He went out and did some shopping yesterday. More than he meant. He even purchased a new pair of sunglasses. It is December, but snow can be blinding while driving through Austria.

At least the car doesn't look too bad. He'll be fine as long as he's sitting in his car. He is now like those news anchors on television: head and shoulders looking normal, but disaster below the desk level. The TV Centaurs.

*

It's been long. He must be careful when talking to his old friends. It's been too long. Almost twenty years since he'd left, the war was still on at the time, and now they're already thinking about a new one. Crazy tribes.

The life that he is living now and what they live there, what he's been through and what they've been through – it is so different it can hardly fit into one languge. They'd been bombed over there. He'd been worried. Worried and bombed don't compare. He's an expert in network security. Some of the programmes he had created – he can't even talk about those. Not that anyone would understand. If he told them what it really was, they'd think it was a condom for digital dicks.

He'll be lonely there. Was Dad lonely after Mum was gone? He was surrounded with the family. There was someone to play cards with, someone to talk about politics, about football. There was a circle. And they will be around now, the lot. He could imagine – the advisers, the usurpers, the brainwashers. Everyone will know, everyone with a solution.

It wasn't Dad, it was he that will be lonely. Okay, Penn is there, but still.

That is to be expected, no? To leave means to forfeit your right to the place. You get up and leave your seat on the park bench. You can't expect it to be waiting for you in twenty years. Even the bench would be gone.

One more hour, then a break, and then south.

*

In arts, time can be stretched when needed. Artists control the flow to show their virtuosity through a long description of a tragic scene, or a slow motion, or a multiple exposition, or long notes...

In life, time can be stretched even further. What should've been hours can last for months, and a single event can extend over years, over a whole life. Pain controls time in life. But none of this applies in death. Death is faster than word, than sound. You just see a large black shape hurling towards you, and that's it.

NATALIE HAYNES

The Two Penelopes

1
October

Penny sat in an ugly chair, her elbows balanced on its wooden arms, her skinny denim legs clashing against its lurid green seat. She held up the red nest of wool, trying to help the old lady – whose name she didn't know – to unravel its most persistent knots. She had been visiting the old people's home for a couple of months now, and she still only knew a handful of its residents by name: Eric, who was sitting over by the window, muttering to himself as he filled in today's crossword; Alice, in front of the mirror, whose faintly blue hair was being teased into waves by a young man as they gossiped about two new nurses. Harvey was outside in the garden, his hands bunched in the pockets of his threadbare cardigan. He was clearly on the prowl for a cigarette, but the gardener simply shrugged and held out his hands. And the old lady in front of Penny, whatever she was called, who sat in an upright chair, knitting bag at her feet, thick glasses on her nose, hair whisked into shape. She was hunched over, as though she had once been tall and it had embarrassed her. Her mauve cardigan was bobbled with age, obscuring the intricate lace pattern which must have once looked very smart.

Penny came to the home on Wednesday afternoons, as squarely in the middle of the week as she could muster. Other people always said that weekends were the hardest, and she nodded and agreed because it wasn't a conversation she wished to have again. But Penelope had found she didn't mind the weekends so much. They were easy to pack with errands. Oliver had been away for so many weekends that she had practised living through them. The rest of the week was much harder. She felt a tug on her right wrist.

'You have to keep your arms up, dear,' said the old lady. 'Or I can't see which way the yarn is going.'

'Sorry,' Penny raised her arms again, feeling her shoulders rise with them.

'Penny for your thoughts,' said the lady. 'Do people say that to you all the time? They've always said it to me.'

'I was just thinking about filling time,' said Penny. 'That's all hobbies are, isn't it? Ways to fill time.'

'I suppose they are. Although knitting is different from a crossword, isn't it?' The lady tilted her head towards Eric, whose creased brow suggested that the crossword was eluding him today. 'I mean, at the end of it, you have something you didn't have before. And it's a good way to use up old wool, like this.'

'What are you planning to knit, when we've finished winding the wool?' asked Penny.

'I don't know,' replied the old lady, her thin lips pursing as she considered the question. 'I know what I'd like to knit, but I'm not sure how to go about it.' She reached into her wool bag, and offered Penny a slightly battered magazine. 'Look.'

Penny reached over and took it from the woman's hand. The skin was so thin and dry, it felt like the crisp leaves which had crunched underfoot as Penny walked through the grounds this morning. She had always loved Bournville for its trees. She loved the sticky pavements, when the linden trees shed their sap in the spring. And she loved the thick carpeting of leaves which appeared every autumn.

'Page 62,' said the lady, and Penny flicked through until she saw the story.

'Yarn-bombing?'

The lady smiled. 'Exactly.'

Penny scanned the article. Yarn-bombing, it transpired, was knitting at its most political. Penny realised she had never previously considered knitting to be political at all. But here were pictures to prove it. She read about groups of women who met to knit slogans or make jokes in rainbow colours, before wrapping them around lamp-posts or festooning them across streets, like bunting. 'Sorry,' read one banner. 'The lifestyle you ordered is out of stock'. Next to it stood a bronze statue of a man in Victorian garb, now wearing a bright blue scarf, picked out with yellow dots. 'Yarn-bombing is for fun or mischief,' Penny read. 'Often both.'

She looked up at the old lady, who was still smiling. 'What do you think?' she asked.

Penny thought for a moment. 'You'll need someone to help. No disrespect intended, but I'm not convinced you could climb a ladder while carrying a big woollen banner.'

The lady nodded.

'I'm assuming you have a ladder,' she said. 'Can you knit?'

2
November

The two women sat at the table by the windows, looking at their work in the cold autumn sun. Their stash now filled a large plastic crate, but still there was more wool to wind.

'Where does it all come from?' asked Penny.

'They're old sweaters,' the lady replied. 'I've been unravelling them since I got here, two years ago.'

'Why?'

'I found them when I cleared out my house,' said the old lady. 'Oh, I hope you never have to do that. I hope you die when you're still healthy.'

Penny looked surprised.

'You know what I mean,' said the lady. 'Not soon. Just, don't get like me.' She pointed a gnarled finger, bent like a tree trunk on a bare hillside at her thick glasses. 'Half-blind, arthritic hands, crumbling spine.'

'Is that why you had to move in here?' Penny asked.

'My son wanted me to move in, when my husband died. He lives in Australia, you see. My son. And he didn't want to have to worry about me, that's what he said.'

'I'm sorry.'

'I don't mind. Well, I still think of some of my ornaments.' The old lady's eyes filled with sudden tears, and Penny felt herself flush with embarrassment. Was she crying, or was it just eye strain from peering at the tangled yarn?

'I meant – about your husband,' she said.

'Oh, don't be sorry about him.' The lady dug into her sleeve for a crumpled tissue. 'Ghastly man. No-one would miss him. Least of all me, who'd had to put up with him for a lot longer than the rest of you.' She blew her nose, and dabbed at her watery eyes. 'And don't look so stricken. I should never have married him. But I was so young after the war, you see. And men were in short supply. So I leapt into it, thinking I was the luckiest girl in England. And then found out that I was just like all the others. But by then, of course, it was too late.'

'Why didn't you leave him?' Penny said.

'Well, we had Colin, and I suppose that distracted me for a while. And he wasn't a cruel man, just an awful philanderer. Once I'd accepted that, it wasn't so bad. At least he was away a lot, at all those conferences he pretended to be going to.'

'I mean, why didn't you leave him when Colin had grown up?' Penny didn't like to ask the old lady her age, but she was well over eighty, at a guess. So her son must have left home – what? – forty years before his father died.

'I don't know,' the old lady's shoulders twitched, as though she were trying to shrug but could not. 'I suppose I thought Colin would be upset. I don't know why: he hardly ever mentioned his father in his letters and phone calls. And then he met Anne-Marie and they moved to the other side of the world. And in my head – I know this makes me sound quite mad – he was still a little boy, really. I knew perfectly well that he was a grown man, and married and a father himself. But because I didn't see him for a year or two at a time, my mind kept sliding back to how I remembered him, I suppose. I kept thinking of his face when he was little – he used to blush easily, like you, and his freckles would suddenly get lost in a sea of red – and I thought I couldn't possibly do anything to make him unhappy. But, do you know, I don't think he would have minded one bit? He and Anne-Marie didn't come back for Graham's funeral, you know. She was very unwell at the time – she's in remission now – and they sent the loveliest flowers. But not for him, for his father, I mean. They sent the flowers for me. Beautiful gerberas, orange and pink, not a bit like funeral flowers. And it was really only then that I realised that Colin didn't like his father any more than I did.'

'So you decided to unravel all his jumpers?' Penny asked.

'Not all of them,' the old lady smiled through cracked lips. 'Just the ones I knitted for him, when we were first married. I found them all in a drawer in the spare bedroom, you see. I thought he'd thrown them out years ago. And I thought back to the girl who made them: so hopeful and silly, with no idea that the reason her big, important husband was away all the time was because he was having a fling with every girl in the typing pool. And first I thought I'd burn them all in the garden, but then I thought that would smell awful and what if a hedgehog wandered in and got cooked? It's hardly his fault that my husband was such a bore, is it?'

'No, I suppose it isn't.'

'So I decided to bring them all with me in a suitcase, and turn them into something else. Something that made people smile.'

'Have you decided what we're going to make?'

3
December

Penny was in the residents' room before she knew anything was wrong. No-one had said anything to her as she signed herself in. Perhaps they hadn't noticed how much time she'd been spending with the old lady. It was Eric – looking up in annoyance from his crossword when Penny asked him where the lady was – who told her she was ill. Penny took her knitting bag along the corridor to room 23, hoping they could continue the project. She knocked on the door and opened it.

The old lady's eyes were closed. Her white hair was flattened against her skull, and her bird-like ribs moved only slightly. Her pulse feathered through a vein on her neck. Penny felt tears spill from her eyes, as she dropped her bag on a chair. She walked towards the bed and spoke softly.

'Hello,' she said. 'Penelope? It's Penny here, your knitting partner. Remember?'

The old lady gave no sign of recognition. Her thin, ragged breathing stayed the same.

'I brought my knitting,' said Penny. 'I was looking forward to seeing your designs. Did you manage to do any, before you were ill?' She looked around the room, helplessly. She didn't want to go riffling through the old lady's things.

'I've been looking forward to seeing you all week,' she said. 'I wanted to talk to you about, well, about everything, I suppose. I wanted to talk to you about me.'

A carer bustled in behind her, carrying a pile of towels.

'Are you chatting to her?' he asked. 'That's great.'

'Is she...?' Penny couldn't finish the sentence.

'Maybe,' he said. 'Are you family?'

'No, just a visitor.'

'There's no 'just' about it,' he said. 'No-one else has come to see her in as long as I can remember. I don't know if she can hear you, but it's better to try than not. I'll not disturb you again till four,' he said, and bustled out again.

'He seems nice,' Penny said. 'Anyway, I wanted to talk to you about your husband. You're so matter-of-fact about him. About his affairs, I mean. And I wanted to know how you got there. You never asked me why I started coming to visit you, because I think you knew something must have happened. I wonder if it's often like that with volunteers. I wonder if everyone does it because they just want something to do, and someone to talk to. That's an awful thought, isn't it? All those volunteers trying to make themselves feel better. But maybe it doesn't matter why we come here, so long as we come. Do you think that's right?'

Penny felt foolish, asking questions of a woman who was apparently unconscious, but she persevered.

'I'm lonely, you see. It's such an unfashionable thing to say, isn't it? I used to feel rather envious of you all, living here together. I live alone. Work from home. I can go days without seeing someone. Sometimes I order books and things, just so I can talk to a delivery man for a minute in a day or two's time. Did you guess my husband had left me? I don't think I mentioned it, but perhaps you could tell. And when you spoke about Graham – that was your late husband's name, wasn't it? – I envied you more than ever. Because you just didn't seem to care at all. And I want so much to be like you. I want things to hurt less. I told a friend that, and she said I was wishing myself dead. She said that's the only time nothing hurts. But then I met you, and you just didn't seem to care. And I wished I could be like that. He's left me for someone else, and I don't even know her name. He wouldn't tell me. And I spent – honestly – weeks trying to decide whether it is better or worse to be able to put a name to the person who has stolen my life. I couldn't think about anything else, really. And then I met you, and you were so tough. And I came back today to work on our yarn-bombing and to ask you how you did it. Was it just time? How long did it take, not to care?'

The old lady didn't respond. Penny rubbed her knuckles on her eyelids, and stood up. She walked over to the window and gazed out at the leafless trees and muddy lawn. She had the uncomfortable sensation that she was asking questions to which she already knew the answers.

'I don't know what you want to do with our knitting,' she said, without turning around. 'I had a few ideas. I thought we could cover the sign outside. You know where it says 'Long-leaved Tree Rest Home' on the driveway? I've always thought that was an odd name. I thought perhaps we could do something with that.'

Penny turned away from the window to look at the old lady but still, she hadn't moved. Penny took her papery hand, and found it surprisingly warm. She sat in silence until the carer opened the door again.

'Still here?' he asked.

'I suppose I should be going,' said Penny. She let go of the lady's hand as gently as she could. She leaned over the bed, and kissed her on the forehead. 'Goodbye,' she said.

4
January

Colin felt cold and queasy in equal measure. It was jetlag, he supposed, mingled with guilt that he hadn't seen his mother before she died, and the fact that it was well below freezing and he didn't have a winter coat. It was a virus, they'd told him. These things just happen to people as old as Penelope. No-one's fault. A good way to go.

He wanted nothing more than to crawl into an airport hotel and sleep for a week. But he trudged his way to the car rental company, and picked up an anonymous car. He started to drive towards Bournville, trying to recognise buildings from his childhood. It was implausibly difficult: new blocks of flats had sprung up all along Bristol Road, and something strange had happened by the University. Was it possible a whole new road had been built while he'd been away? None of these observations lessened his guilt. He'd been gone for so long the whole city had shifted, and he hadn't even known. His mother hadn't mentioned it, of course.

He found himself on a strange new route, driving past the back of the Queen Elizabeth Hospital. At least, he hoped that's where he was, but the hospital now looked like a ship, leaning up towards an enormous prow. Nothing was as he remembered. He turned right and drove down another forgotten street, before finally recognising the rest home ahead of him.

He indicated and turned into the driveway, which was lined with black trees, devoid of life. He frowned. What did that say? The car staggered to a halt, as he tried to slow down but stalled instead.

The home's sign looked oddly fuzzy. And whatever the place was called – Colin flushed to realise he had forgotten that too – he was sure it wasn't 'Penelope's Last Stand,' as it now unevenly claimed.

He got out of the car to look more closely. The original sign had been completely obscured by woollen squares, each one containing a letter. Wound around the signposts were two long strips, like scarves, made up of bright pink and orange knitted flowers. Looking up the drive, he saw there was a knitted flower pinned to every tree. Was this a thing people did in Britain now? His mother had always loved knitting, he knew that. Had the staff decorated the sign in her honour? It couldn't be for his benefit: no-one knew he was coming until they called two nights ago – it felt like weeks had passed since then – and told him she had died. It was for her, then. Nothing to do with him.

He dug around and pulled out his phone, taking a

picture of the whole strange scene. He would send it to Anne-Marie later. Nothing felt real until he had told his wife. He looked again at the letters of his mother's name and realised he was smiling.

DAVID CALCUTT

The Old Man in the Garden

He was trying to get his breath, that first good breath, but it wouldn't come because there was something holding him down, and a heaviness in his chest that he had to push through to get at the breath. It was like a man fallen overboard in black night into a black sea, struggling to fight his way up again while the bottom of the sea grabbed at his feet and tried to pull him down. It was always like that, and he kicked against it, or something kicked inside him, and finally he got it, that first good breath, and he took it in, deep, and let it out again, long and slow, and it was always like that. Always as if it might be the last. But it wasn't the last, not this time, and here he was now safe again in the garden chair on the lawn, with his head towards the sun and the heat full on his face, and with the sweet, strong smell of mown grass and the sound of the shears clipping the hedge.

It was all settling itself back into shape, and he sat, letting it settle, letting the breathing come without having to think too much about it. Then he eased his weight up a little out of the chair and made a half-turn, shielding his eyes and squinting through the glare towards the sound of the shears. There was a shadowy figure, and he tried to make out who it was but he couldn't. Then a name came to him and he spoke it, "Richard?" and he pushed himself up higher from the chair, his breath wheezing in his chest with the effort, and extended a hand into the brightness. But a voice spoke out of the shadow,

'No, not Richard,' and he let his hand fall back, an emptiness slipping out between his fingers. 'Who, then…?'

'Tony,' said the voice.

'Tony,' he said. 'Oh.' Then, still leaning forward, squinting towards the shadow, 'What are you doing here?'

Tony didn't answer straight away.

'I'm doing your garden.'

'What for?' he said.

'You asked me to. It needs doing.'

He listened to the snipping of the shears.

'I used to have a man who came and did the garden.'

'He hasn't been for a long time,' said Tony.

'What happened to him?'

'He stopped coming.'

He frowned, perplexed, and then the shears stopped and he remembered something.

'You're staying here, aren't you?'

'Yes.'

'Just you.'

'Just me.'

'How long for?'

'I don't know yet.'

'And you're doing the garden,' he said.

'Yes. I'm doing the garden.'

The clipping of the shears started again and they seemed to be clipping away at something inside him so that he was falling or floating, everything coming loose and tumbling away, but then it settled again and he relaxed back into his chair, his eyes closed.

'Better get on with it, then,' he said, though the words, if actually spoken at all, came as a breathy gasp that trembled insect-like upon his lips, and fluttered away unheard to become one with the gentle humming and buzzing of the sunlight.

Tony climbed down from the step ladder, holding the shears in one hand, then dropped them onto the grass. He stretched, arching his back and shoulders, and felt the sharp twist in the bottom of his spine that would become a knot of pain bunched and throbbing there by the end of the day. As for in the morning. Feeling his age, his years. Not a young man anymore. But here, back in the garden, a child again. He looked down at what he'd cut. Spiky twists of bramble and briar, dog-rose with its vicious, fang-like thorns, a wicked tangle of some kind of creeper. It was a good job he'd found those old gardening gloves in the shed. A bit small for him, probably his mother's. Better than nothing, though. Tear his hands to ribbons. He stooped and carefully gathered up the cuttings, and carried them, holding them out and away from his body, to the top corner of the garden by the fence, and dropped them onto the compost pile. And there let them rot. Or burn.

The breathing was still easy and the heat was inside his shirt like a flame and under his eyelids where it made spangled, kaleidoscopic patterns and he felt he was watching them and amongst them at the same time. Faces came and went and came again, too swiftly for him to put a name to before they changed shape and became something else. There was no sound inside the heat. He no longer felt cumbersome or heavy, although his feet were throbbing a little inside his shoes a long way off. If he could just find the strength to sit up and lean forward and untie the laces, take them off, take his socks off as well and feel the warm sand beneath his feet. Listen to the big rollers coming in over the beach down in the bay. His happiest time out there. Watching the sea-lions playing in the waves and the pelicans flying low across the surface of the sea. Early morning, the happiest time. He could almost believe he was there again but it was grass not sand beneath his feet, and he was in his garden. But what was Richard doing here? He called out.

'What are you doing here, Richard?'

And Tony called back.

'I'm not Richard.'

He let what the voice had said sink in. Not Richard, no.

Tony, here doing his garden. In this heat. What for? Nobody had asked him to. He shifted uncomfortably in his chair, turning his head to the side, trying to escape the sun full on his face. The garden didn't need doing, it was all right, and he'd be all right if he could just be left alone, if he could just be given a bit of peace and quiet. But there wasn't any, neither peace nor quiet, not with the sound of those shears clipping away, snip, snip, snip. And this heat, he could hardly breathe, it was like being wrapped in bandages from head to foot. He struggled to be free of them, twisting his body round. And then he thought, with sudden savagery, and with such force that he might have said it aloud, 'It'll be the bloody death of me!'

As he leaned over to make a cut on the far side of the hedge, he felt the acid rise through into his throat, bringing the nausea with it, and he shut his eyes and swallowed it down, burning. He stood on the ladder, head bent forward, waiting for it to pass, then placed the shears on top of the hedge and took the half-empty bottle of water out of one of the zipped sidepockets of his trousers and took a long drink. He screwed the cap on and put the bottle back in the pocket and picked up the shears and carried on cutting. At least there wasn't much more to do now. Just a little while longer and it would be done with. Until he had to do it again. Or find another gardener. But for some reason it was difficult finding another gardener. Either they didn't answer the messages he left, or if they did, they didn't want to take on the work. So he'd have to do it again himself. Unless he had it all taken out. He'd thought about that before. Find someone to come and cut it all down and put up a wooden fence. A good wooden fence. There was more than a few days' work in that, they'd take on that, all right, it would pay them to do that job. It would take some getting up, though. They'd have to get down to the roots, dig those up. And the hedge had been here a long time. The first thing the old man had planted after he'd put down the lawn. That was a long time ago. Long enough for the roots to go really deep. Right down. How far? he wondered. How deep do these roots go? Down to the mineshafts maybe on which this house is built. The whole smoke-choked town. Garden of earthly delights. A crumbling foundation. Would all fall someday, slide down into that sulphurous pit? The devil's heartland. And raise them, the dead-undead, restless spirits of the whole brood, the ghosts he carried within him. Mother. And you, my underworld brother. They fed on his blood.

He cut through a thick rose stalk that grew almost vertically up from the hedge then made a few more cuts and snips and he was done. He looked along the hedge. It was as good as he was going to make it. The sun was hot on the back of his neck and the tops of his arms and he could feel the sweat sticky under his tee shirt. He closed the shears and dropped them onto the lawn then gathered up the last of the cuttings and dropped those as well. Then he climbed down the ladder and picked them up and carried them over to the compost heap.

He woke with a bad taste in his mouth, a sour taste. And something was brushing against his face, like cobwebs, and he flicked at them with his hand. He opened his eyes into the glare of sunlight and there was Richard's face, looking down at him. Somebody spoke. He rose in the chair, leaning towards the face, the voice.

'What's that you say, Richard?'

'I said do you want me to burn it?' said Tony.

He screwed up his eyes, trying to see through the glare. He wasn't sure who he was talking to, and he shook his head, trying to clear it of the tangles of dry thread and dust.

'Burn what?' he said.

'The clippings from the hedge.'

But they wouldn't clear and he found himself brushing again at the air in front of his face with his hands and he couldn't stop them doing that. And someone was speaking to him, 'Are you all right? What is it?' and he could feel them tickling his face, 'What are you doing?' and he brushed at them and brushed them away.

'All right,' he said, then louder, 'It's all right,' and then, tentatively, looking up, 'It's Tony, isn't it?'

'Yes,' said Tony.

'You were saying about the hedge,' he said, and it was coming clearer now. 'The clippings,' he said. 'That's right. Yes, go on, burn them.'

'I wasn't being serious,' said Tony.

'What do you mean?' he said, and now there was a fuzziness again at the edges.

'About burning the clippings. Not with everything so dry. It's not safe. The whole place could go up.'

He looked out at the yellow, withered grass of the lawn on which he sat in his chair, the wilted flowers along the border, their curled and cracked leaves, and with a delicate movement lifted his hand as if to brush away once more the dust and shadows. He raised a finger, pointing, trembling, then let the hand fall back into his lap.

'I smelled the cut grass...' he said. Then the sourness was in his mouth and he felt his voice when he spoke dry and flaking on his lips.

'I'm thirsty. Can you get me something to drink?'

'You've already got one,' said Tony, and he picked up a glass of flat lemonade from the side of the chair and held it out to him. He took it, felt the warm glass between his fingers, the warm liquid on his tongue. He took another sip and sat, holding the glass at an angle in his hand. He looked up again at Tony.

'What did you say it for if you weren't being serious?' he said.

'I was having a joke,' said Tony.

'Oh,' he said, then, as Tony moved away, he called out, 'It can go up, for all I care. Burn it. Burn it all up and me with it.'

He gave a hard, bitter laugh, and spilled some of the lemonade on his trousers. He wiped at it with his free hand then raised the glass and drank from it again, the bittersweet taste in his mouth now, taking the sourness away, and he felt better, and lifted the glass once more and glanced up at the bedroom window.

Standing by the fence at the back of the garden he took a long drag on the cigarette and blew the smoke away from the lawn, over the fence. Looking back then at the compost heap, the fresh cuttings on top and the older, dry stuff piled underneath. It wouldn't take long to catch. He watched the flames crawling among the leaves and grass cuttings, almost invisible in the bright sunlight, the pale smoke curling up, the satisfying crackle of the flames as they burned more fiercely, felt on his hands and face now, then rising suddenly in a rush of heat, catching onto the overhanging branches of the apple tree and spreading quickly through the bushes along the fence, then out over the lawn, a great blaze, consuming all. Burn it all up.

He turned and looked again over the fence at the scrubby patch of wasteland and the estate beyond the wasteland where there had once been open ground rising to the hill overlooking the canal. Standing there that time the three of them above the town and watching the sheet of fire pour upwards as they opened the foundry doors, the night sky drenched and bloody and melting back into the furnace, and his father saying to them, 'That's why we came to live up here, to get away from all that.' He looked up, squinting. A swift fell with a high thin scream across the sky, and was gone, and then there was only the sky's relentless and formless blue. You don't get away. No matter how far you think you may have travelled, nor who you were or tried or pretended to be, you turn a sudden corner in yourself and you're back and you've never been gone, and you can smell it and taste it, the smell and taste of your own blood, and the cramped and crooked streets too grown crooked in your blood. No way out of them, except that one way, and you found that, brother, or it found you, and you jumped and tumbled all the way out, through the blue sky and the blank space between the eyes. And now I have to be both of us.

The cigarette was almost burned down and he'd hardly smoked it. He took a final drag then bent down and stubbed it out carefully on a large stone, tearing the end off with his moistened fingers and putting the remains under the stone. Then he stepped around the compost heap and back onto the lawn. His father was looking up at the back of the house and his glass was tilted in his hand and there was a dark patch on the front of his trousers where the lemonade had spilled. He reached down and took the glass from his father's hand and put it on the grass beside the chair.

'What is it?' he said.

There was an absence in his father's face.

'I don't know,' he said, and shook his head and made that odd brushing movement again with his hand. 'I thought… I don't know.' He looked up towards the house again, and he turned and looked up as well. He heard his father's voice behind him, cracked and faltering. 'His bedroom window,' he said. 'There was someone there.' He looked long and hard at the shadow in the window then turned back.

'There's no one there,' he said.

'It was just then,' said his father. 'I looked up and I saw… somebody up there.' He was leaning towards him with both hands raised in a gesture of entreaty, of appeal. His eyes were red-rimmed and moist. The clothes he wore were old and stained and shabby, and too many for the heat, and they were worn past wearing out, and the man himself too.

'There's nobody there,' he said again. 'It's all right.'

His father nodded, letting his hands fall, then shook his head and lifted one hand again to press a finger and thumb to the bridge of his nose. He stood looking down at him, not knowing what to say, never knowing what to say.

'I've got to go out now,' he said. 'The hedge is done. I'll be back later.'

His father took his hand from his face.

'You'll be back,' he said.

'Yes,' he said. 'I'll be back. That's what I said.'

His father sat back in his chair. The sun was already drying the spilled lemonade on his trousers. His body sagged, the jowls loose about his neck, eyes sunken beneath their lids. As he will appear on the hospital bed beneath the smoothed and neatly folded back sheet. Sitting alone with him for long minutes listening to the silence then reaching out to touch the mottled hand resting long-fingered upon the sheet, and feeling the utter coldness of that hand, that was no less cold than his own heart. He turned away from it and went towards the house.

There was the sun on his face and he could hear the gentle humming of it and see it golden through his shut eyelids. Then someone was there and he opened his eyes to see a shadow standing over him. He couldn't tell who it was and he began to sit forward in the chair and to speak a name but there was a heaviness in his chest and the breathing wouldn't come and then the shadow was gone. He sat back again in his chair. He was comfortable and his breathing was fine. He didn't want to get up. There was the smell of mown grass. He didn't want ever to get up again. There was the sun on his face.

REFLECTIONS

YASMIN ALI

My interest in Greek mythology began with an important Birmingham figure, Charles Kingsley, a former President of The Birmingham and Midland Institute in the 1870s. Kingsley's children's book, *The Heroes*, was given to me when I was 5 years old by my head teacher at Cotteridge Primary School, to read in hospital as I recovered from open heart surgery. Precocious reading, you might think, but I loved it.

By my teens I was reading the real thing, including the *Odyssey*. But that's where it stayed, a part of my schooldays, until I was asked to contribute a story to this project. I re-read Homer, did a little research, and my adult reaction to these tales was very different from my memories. Two things struck me. As a writer, I admired the way Homer constructed the *Odyssey*. I was also fascinated by the world view of the ancient Greeks. As a way of making sense of human experience it had a lot of resonance for the contemporary world. For are we not at the mercy of capricious gods? Bankers, oligarchs, tech billionaires, media tycoons – without a second thought they can bestow good fortune, or more likely, derail our lives.

DAVID CALCUTT

In the final book of the *Odyssey*, Odysseus, having returned home, killed the suitors, regained his home, and been reunited with Penelope, goes to see his father, Laertes, in Laertes' garden. It's his final meeting in the book. The story's over, and there's nothing more to happen but for Laertes to die and for Odysseus to settle down and grow old. This meeting between father and son was the starting point for my story. I also wanted to write about the idea that there seem to be two people called Odysseus, the one who has adventures abroad, and the one who comes home, and tells stories about the one who has the adventures, and that through his storytelling and constant shape-shifting, brings about a deliberate confusion of identity. Maybe he isn't even the real Odysseus, but an imposter, and the real one is still out there, ceaselessly wandering through the shadowlands of myth, a figure eternally lost, eternally longed-for. And it's these two versions of Odysseus, the one dead-but-alive, the other living-but-dead, and their relationship to the old man, Laertes, at the end of his life, that form the basis for this new story.

ELISABETH CHARIS

Being new to the *Odyssey* I was surprised to discover a protagonist apparently weak and unable to face his responsibilities instead of the majestic hero I had expected. The character's constant pitching of himself as a champion, cunning and capable, seems so at odds with the poor decisions he repeatedly makes and his alleged lack of agency. I wanted to address this. What kind of man would he be in the modern world, I wondered, and what kind of circumstances could make him incapable of proactive decisions? Homer has him trapped and tormented by his stay with 'the beautiful goddess', Calypso, for example; something I found implausible and dishonest.

I set out to address these questions and reframe his struggle as entirely personal. In exploring his character, though, I found myself surprised at how easily I mapped the ideas of fate and destiny into his world. I hoped to show him as free but discovered quickly that people can feel themselves bound by expectations just as much as by any god's manoeuvring.

LINDSEY DAVIS

I didn't have long to write this story, so was very grateful that Homer had done most of the creative work. I felt a bit nervous about tampering with such famous and wonderful poetry though. We could select which part of the *Odyssey* we re-wrote. I was expecting to choose one of the famous incidents involving Odysseus (Nausicaa always seems an interesting girl) but to my own surprise decided that the inspiring of Telemachus by Athene would be easier; our brief was to set the story in the Midlands, and Birmingham is rather lacking in 'wine dark sea'!

I wanted to stick fairly closely to the original. That way, modern readers who know Homer could enjoy the comparisons, but I would make it readable for everyone else too. I had such fun finding modern equivalents, like 'texting' as a means of summoning the gods, and making a modern corporate environment fit rural Ithaca, right down to the man who says he can read a balance sheet (instead of resorting to prophesy). I particularly enjoyed the idea that Penelope thwarts the Suitors by bringing in management consultants; I'm sure we've all been victims of that.

KIT DE WAAL

I've never been commissioned to write anything before so I jumped at the chance to be part of the *A Midlands Odyssey*, without really thinking it through and only began to engage with the brief after I'd said yes. I didn't know the *Odyssey* though fragments had survived from school and bits of films I'd seen, so I came to the story almost cold. I chose not to read any interpretations and academic studies but read my part of the poem to see what I made of it and found that there were parallels with something I already had in mind, sitting on my shoulder, waiting to be written. It was about a man and a laundrette and contained a lot of the elements that fitted

Nausica's story – journeying, water, desire and restraint. Although my chapter is written from a male perspective, I think it is Nausica's story and every woman's story; mother, carer, sister, confessor, lover, wife – these are the roles we adopt in life, often within a single relationship. I hope I have done us justice.

NATALIE HAYNES

I have always fought shy of reworking Penelope's story, because Margaret Atwood pretty much nailed it with her wonderful *Penelopiad*. But this was an irresistible opportunity. I knew I wanted to find a way of telling an updated version of Penelope's delaying strategy: weaving a shroud for her father -in-law by day, and then unweaving it again at night (she has told her suitors that she will only consider marrying one of them when the shroud is finished, trying to buy time for her husband Odysseus – believed by the suitors to be long dead – to return).

So I hit upon the idea of an old woman unravelling jumpers she once knitted for someone she loved. I wanted to give readers the idea that the process of making and unmaking was delaying something. For my Penelope, it was postponing death rather than an unwanted marriage.

My friend Nora is a thoroughly mischievous yarn-bomber. I wouldn't have thought of it if she hadn't mailed me pictures of her most recent projects. So my thanks to her. I hope Penny joins a gang of like-minded guerrilla knitters like Nora, who will remind her that friendship is a balm for ragged souls.

CHARLIE HILL

When I was approached to contribute to this anthology, I knew straight away that I would like to write a thoroughly modern story, one that focussed on the interior life of Odysseus rather than something that happened in the *Odyssey*. After speaking with Polly I decided to re-imagine the moment when Odysseus weeps as a bard recounts the story of the Trojan horse. As a gap in the drive of the narrative – however small – this seemed to be the perfect subject matter. I wrote the story as a stream of consciousness, partly because this is a quintessentially modern idiom, and partly because its conversational style echoes the informality of the oral tradition from which the *Odyssey* emerged. I tried – as always – to be playful, but there were limits to my ambition. There was no way I could attempt a modern re-setting of Homer without a nod to James Joyce for example; equally, I thought that to try and make reference or pay homage to *Ulysses* too explicitly was a mug's game. So I contented myself with creating an Odysseus who shares some of the corporeal directness of Joyce...

RICHARD HOUSE

I read the *Odyssey* as a boy, in some doctored version which omitted the Underworld section, in which Ulysses summons the dead through blood rites and sacrifice. In this section he seeks advice on why he has not been able to return home, and what he needs to do to achieve this. More significantly, he learns of the death of his mother, and has difficult encounters with the dead from Troy – most notably Achilles. It is the most remarkable episode in the entire narrative, not only is it spectacular (the way in which the ghosts must be summoned to a trench of blood), but it threatens to undermine not only the *Odyssey*, but the *Iliad*. Achilles is clear – all of this slaughter, all of this war, and what was it for? In my version I have a character called Buzz returning home to Birmingham. It's part of a larger narrative I'm currently writing. Buzz is returning home from Laos, which, like Troy, has suffered sustained assault. From 1964 - 1973 over 270 million cluster bombs were dropped on the Plain of Jars. That's the equivalent of one

B-52 bomb-load every 8 minutes for 9 years. Over one third of these bombs did not detonate, and are still, even now, causing injury and retarding economic development. Buzz has his own history, we meet him on his last night in Laos. He's burdened by events that have occurred during his time as a volunteer, and troubled by his earlier volunteering for people with HIV/AIDS. Much of this will be developed in a longer narrative. It has been useful to look for commonalities: an absence, an isolated man, a return home, blood, a trench, the prescience of the dead, the need to confront a past in order to move forward. Like Ulysses, Buzz has questions. Unlike Ulysses, he does not want to return home, and his dead refuse to speak – but they need to be challenged.

PAUL McDONALD

My story is based on Odysseus's encounter with the Cyclops, Polyphemus. I was drawn to it because the trick Odysseus plays on the Cyclops is one of the few comic moments in the story, and it is sometimes cited as one of the oldest jokes in literature. The episode reveals the hero's cunning, but also his vanity and stupidity. Ultimately it doesn't turn out well for him at all: Polyphemus is the son of the god Poseidon, and Odysseus's actions leave him subject to divine vengeance. As anyone who lives in Walsall will tell you, divine vengeance is enough to ruin your entire day. I was looking for a way into the story while the 2014 World Cup was in progress, and the idea of constructing Odysseus as a football hooligan struck me as an amusing challenge. I rename him Keith and present him as a Walsall estate agent whose glory-seeking finds an outlet in his role as leader of a hooligan firm; my Polyphemus I call Kyrylo (the Ukrainian form of Cyril) and he's a Kiev policeman whose dad has a lot of clout. I tell myself repeatedly that Homer would have been proud.

DRAGAN TODOROVIC

Nostos, homecoming, is one of the key words of Homer's Greece. Everything was slower then – wars and journeys especially. A man leaving home to go to war or travel could be away for months, if not years.

Who is the man that comes home? Being an exile myself for the past 20 years, I claim the right to answer: we die as soon as we leave. Society, like gas, tends to spread and fill the space emptied by someone's departure.

My Ulix (he doesn't have the name in the story, but here it is) is a man who can clearly be very successful in this world, who can change places, ideas, lovers, but has that ultimate sorrow of someone who is separated from his family, his roots, his language. Penelope is his best friend, and he is very loyal to her, which I believe is a more plausible version of a relationship twenty years old. And, like the ancient original, Ulix creates his own Trojan horse, but it is now a digital version.

You see, thousands of years have passed and not much has changed. Except the river and us, and that is why the same water cannot quench our thirst twice.

BIOGRAPHIES

YASMIN ALI has been writing for over 20 years. In the early 1990s she was a contributor to a pioneering book *Refusing Holy Orders* (Virago 1992) written by founder members of Women Against Fundamentalism. She has written about the politics of gender and ethnicity, and also about social policy. However, it is only within the last few years that Yasmin has begun to write fiction, contributing to short story anthologies, writing a play in collaboration with an oral history project, Cymru Ddu, and other creative projects. She is completing a novel. Yasmin is a member of Tindal Street Fiction Group.

DAVID CALCUTT is a playwright, poet and novelist. He has written many plays and adaptations for BBC radio and the theatre, and has also worked as a writer and director in a variety of community settings. He has published four novels and several plays with Oxford University Press for children and teenagers, and four pamphlets of poetry. His recent work includes four street-theatre plays, a reminiscence play for Stratford Literature Festival, a carnival procession, and *The Life and Times of the Tat Man*, a one-man play. He is working on some new short stories and a novel.

ELISABETH CHARIS, a Room 204 writer for Writing West Midlands, is a thinker, writer, teacher, facilitator and permaculturalist currently living on her boat in England. She mostly writes reviews and poetry though is also working on a novel. In 2013 she was shortlisted to be Birmingham Poet Laureate. This was her first short story. Elisabeth is interested in the transformative possibilities of creative writing and often works with marginalised or vulnerable young people and adults. She enjoys working with artists from other disciplines and, in particular, exploring the shared language between photographic and word art. She is a member of the Tindal Street Fiction Group.

JONATHAN DAVIDSON is Chief Executive of Writing West Midlands, the region's literature development agency. He is involved in a range of literature activities, both through Writing West Midlands and independently.

LINDSEY DAVIS is best known for Roman detective, Marcus Didius Falco. She has also written *Rebels and Traitors* and a Quickread, set in the English Civil War, and *Master and God*, about paranoid Emperor Domitian. Her new series about Flavia Albia started with *The Ides of April* in 2013. *Enemies at Home* was published in 2014, with a third to come. Her books are translated and have been dramatized on BBC Radio 4. Her awards include the Premio Colosseo (from the city of Rome), the Barcelona International Historical Novel Prize and the Crimewriters' Cartier Diamond Dagger for lifetime achievement.

KIT DE WAAL was born in Moseley Birmingham, one of five children of an Irish mother and Caribbean father. She was second in the Costa Short Story Award (2014), The Bath Short Story Award (2014, is longlisted in The Bristol Prize 2014) and the Leeds Literary Prize (2014). Her writing is published by *Fish* (2011 and 2012), *The Sea in Birmingham* (2013), *The Dying Coalition* (2013) and other publications. She is a member of Tindal Street Fiction Group, Leather Lane Writers and Oxford Narrative Group. She has an MA in Creative Writing, writes and edits non-fiction, and has been short listed for the Leeds Literary Prize.

NATALIE HAYNES lived in Bournville until she was 18. She became a classicist while at school, and it continues to shape her life today. Her first novel, *The Amber Fury*, is a modern-day

Greek tragedy, and her book *The Ancient Guide to Modern Life* compares ancient and modern worlds in the hope of making more sense of them both. She is a frequent contributor to BBC Radio 4, reviewing films, books and plays for Front Row and Saturday Review. Her series *Natalie Haynes Stands Up for the Classics* will return to the airwaves next year.

CHARLIE HILL's writing has been described by *The Observer* as 'rich in wry social commentary', by *The Times* as 'wonderfully observed' and by the *FT* as 'sharp, funny and shrewd'. He is the author of two very different Birmingham-set novels, a political love story called *The Space Between Things* and a satire called *Books*. His stories have been widely published in magazines and journals in print and online and he is working on a short collection called *Post-experimental fictions*.

RICHARD HOUSE is a writer, artist, and lecturer at the University of Birmingham. He is a member of the Chicago-based collaborative, Haha, whose work has appeared at the New Museum, New York; the Museum of Contemporary Art, Chicago; and the Venice Biennale (hahahaha.org) and is the editor of *Fatboy Review*. His recent novel, *The Kills*, was nominated for the Man Booker, Sky Arts South Bank Award, the GC Prize, and the Gordon Burn Prize. Short digital films and audio work associated with *The Kills* can be viewed online at http://www.panmacmillan.com/thekills. He is currently writing a feature film and is working on a new series of novels.

PAUL McDONALD is Senior Lecturer in English at the University of Wolverhampton where he runs the creative writing programme. He is the author of three novels, *Surviving Sting* (2001), *Kiss Me Softly Amy Turtle* (2004), and *Do I Love You?* (2008). His poetry is collected in *The Right Suggestion* (1999), *Catch a Falling Tortoise* (2007), and *An Artist Goes Bananas* (2012). His critical work includes books on

Philip Roth, Joseph Heller, Toni Morrison, American humour, and the philosophy of humour. He takes pleasure in the fact that Googling 'the oldest joke in the world' throws up several hundred pages with his name on.

POLLY STOKER is a PhD student at the University of Birmingham, working under the supervision of Dr Elena Theodorakopoulos in the department of Classics, Ancient History and Archaeology. Her research focuses on reworkings of ancient Greek and Roman literature by contemporary women writers and the ways in which these receptions intersect with feminist theory. Her involvement in this anthology stems from an Arts and Humanities Research Council-funded initiative, entitled Communicating Ancient Greece and Rome (CAGR). Led by the Archive of Performances of Greek and Roman Drama at the University of Oxford, CAGR encourages doctoral students and early career researchers to think about how best to render their work accessible for the wider public, the culmination of which is a public engagement project produced alongside a partner organisation.

DRAGAN TODOROVIC is the author of nine books of non-fiction, poetry and fiction. Some of his books, artistic projects and articles have won international awards. His memoir *The Book of Revenge* (Random House Canada) won The Nereus Writers Trust Non-Fiction Prize. His novel *Diary of Interrupted Days* was shortlisted for several awards, including Commonwealth Writers Prize and the Amazon First Novel Award. His aural essay *In My Language I am Smart*, commissioned for CBC Radio One was published on a CD in 2012. His most recent book is *Little Red Transistor Radio from Trieste* (Nine Arches Press, 2012). Dragan is teaching creative writing at the University of Kent and finishing a new novel.